D1134935

The Case of the Etruscan Treasure

BOOKS BY ROBERT NEWMAN

The Boy Who Could Fly
The Japanese
Merlin's Mistake
The Testing of Tertius
The Shattered Stone
Night Spell
The Case of the Baker Street Irregular
The Case of the Vanishing Corpse
The Case of the Somerville Secret
The Case of the Threatened King
The Case of the Etruscan Treasure

The Case of the Etruscan Treasure

by Robert Newman

Atheneum 1983 *New York*

LIBRARY OF CONGRESS CATALOGING IN PUBLICATION DATA

Newman, Robert.
The case of the etruscan treasure.

SUMMARY: Already in New York with Andrew's actress
mother, Sara and Andrew are curious about
Inspector Wyatt's mysterious case
when he arrives from London.
[1. Mystery and detective stories]   I. Title.
PZ7.N4857Casc   1983   [Fic]   83-2632
ISBN 0-689-30992-9

Published simultaneously in Canada by
McClelland & Stewart, Ltd.
Composition by Service Typesetters, Austin, Texas
Printed and bound
by Fairfield Graphics, Fairfield, Pennsylvania
Designed by Mary Ahern
First Edition

Contents

The Case of the Etruscan Treasure

I

The Visiting Detective

"S.S. *Britannic*," the *New York Times* had said, "arriving from Liverpool, White Star dock, West 10th Street, North River at 9 A.M."

It was only ten minutes after nine according to the clock in the waiting room, and there she was, swinging wide against the tide, then turning, shepherded by the two tugs that pushed and nudged her until she came to rest at her berth alongside the pier.

Sara and Andrew were at the shore-end of the pier behind a barrier guarded by a heavy-set man wearing a black cap with a shiny peak. They had expected to be able to go out onto the pier proper, but the man had stopped them and told them they couldn't without a pass.

"Where do you get a pass?" Andrew had asked.

"Custom House, down at the Battery."

They had been in New York long enough to know where that was. But they also knew that they wouldn't have time enough to get down there and back before the *Brittanic* docked, so they abandoned the idea and remained where they were.

"Why do they call it the North River?" Sara asked. "It's the Hudson, isn't it?"

She had asked the question of Andrew, but the man with the peaked cap turned and said, "I always wondered about that too. Sure it's the Hudson. But this part, along here, is called the North River—I don't know why."

"The early Dutch settlers called it that," said Andrew. "The two rivers they knew best were the Delaware and the Hudson. They called the Delaware the South River so they called this the North. It was only later that they began calling it the Hudson."

"How do you know that?" asked the man.

"I looked it up."

"You're English, aren't you?"

"Yes. But we've been here for quite a while now—over two months."

"Real old settlers yourselves, eh?" he said, grinning.

"I've been meaning to ask you," said Sara, ignoring his joke, "What are those letters for?"

She pointed to the large letters, running from A to Z, that hung from the rafters overhead.

"It's for the passengers' trunks and luggage. When

they're brought off the ship they're put under the first letter of the passenger's last name. Who are you meeting?"

"A friend," said Andrew.

"What's his name?"

"Wyatt."

"Then he'll find his luggage there, under W. A customs inspector will look it over and make sure he's not bringing in anything he shouldn't."

Sara and Andrew carefully avoided looking at one another and hid their smiles. Wyatt as a smuggler was a funny idea.

The ship was tied up now, the gangplank raised and fastened to her side. Longshoremen had gone aboard and some of them had joined the white jacketed stewards and were helping to bring the baggage ashore while others loaded the cranes that were starting to raise the cargo from the hold, swing it out and drop it on the dock.

Andrew and Sara watched the informed visitors who had arrived armed with passes and were now out on the dock waving to the ship's passengers who lined the rails and chatting with them.

There were measured footsteps behind them. They turned and saw an imposing man coming along the dock. He was in his late thirties or early forties, tall and rather portly, with a strong, closely shaven face. He was carefully—almost too immaculately—dressed in a morning coat and striped trousers. His waistcoat was grey and his cravat, of a darker grey, had a pearl stick pin in it. He had one one of those high crowned hats that Americans call a derby rather than a bowler. As he approached the barrier, the man with the peaked cap hurriedly opened the gate and touched his cap. The big man nodded and went through, out onto the dock.

"Did *he* have a pass?" asked Sara. "He didn't show you one."

"What? He didn't need one. That was Dandy Dan Cady."

"Who's that?" asked Andrew.

The man with the peaked cap glanced upward as if the response to such ignorance could well be a bolt of lightning from on high.

"He's boss of the Tenth, Eleventh and Twelfth Wards."

As if to make it clear that no rule or regulation applied to him, Cady took out a cigar and, standing under a No Smoking sign, lit it and tossed the match away. A policeman, standing nearby, carefully avoided looking at him.

Passengers were starting to come down the gangplank.

"There he is!" said Sara.

"Where?"

"Next to the man with the beard, just behind the two ladies with the big hats."

The ladies moved to the left, getting ready to come down the gangplank, and Andrew saw Wyatt standing there, looking relaxed and distinguished in a tweed suit and soft felt hat with a mackintosh thrown over one shoulder.

"The tall chap with the raincoat?" said the man with the peaked cap.

"Yes," said Andrew.

The man looked at Wyatt, then at them.

"He doesn't look like a smuggler and neither do you," he asid, opening the gate. "Go on out there."

"Oh, thank you," said Sara. "Thank you very much!"

They hurried through, walking quickly down the length of the dock. Wyatt was at the top of the gangplank now, looking around as he started down. Putting two fingers to her mouth, Sara whistled one of the loud, shrill urchin whistles that used to shock her mother so. Wyatt heard it over the noise of the cranes, steam winches and baggage trucks, saw them, grinned and waved.

They were still some distance from him when he reached the bottom of the gangplank. A thin man in a dark grey suit was just behind him. He apparently knew Cady, who was standing at the foot of the gangplank, for he nodded to him. Cady nodded back and took a large gold watch from his waistcoat pocket as if to see just how late the ship had been.

Sara and Andrew were running now and, still smiling, Wyatt quickened his pace toward them. Suddenly there was a rattling rumble overhead and a cargo net loaded with heavy crates came crashing down in front of Wyatt, so close to Sara and Andrew that its impact made them stagger.

They stood there for a moment, shocked into stillness and wide-eyed with surprise.

"Sara! Andrew! Are you all right?" called Wyatt. He came running around the pile of crates, his face white, and clutched them each by an arm.

"Yes," said Andrew. "That was a close one."

"Too close," said Wyatt grimly. He turned to the group of men who were hurrying up, picked out one who was carrying an open notebook. "Are you in charge here?"

"Yes. I'm the stevedore boss. Was anyone hurt?"

"By a miracle, no. But another two feet and these children wouldn't just have been hurt. They'd have been killed! Will you tell me how something like that could have happened?"

"I don't know, but I'm going to find out. And take it from me, whoever's responsible won't work on the docks again!" He went hurrying toward the gangplank that led to the foredeck of the ship.

The customs officers had witnessed the near accident and, to make amends, passed Wyatt's baggage—two large valises—without even opening them. Wyatt had just signalled to a porter when two men, one fairly young and the other a bit older, came up the dock toward him.

"Inspector Wyatt?" said the older.

8

"Yes."

"I'm Brenner of the *New York Times* and this is Fitch of the *World*. Can we talk to you for a few minutes?"

"About what?"

"It's not every day we get someone from Scotland Yard over here," said Fitch. "Are you here on a case?"

"I'm afraid I can't answer that. How did you know I was coming?"

"The *World* ran a story about it the other day. Why won't you tell us whether you're here on a case or not?"

"I should think that's obvious."

"You don't have to tell us what the case *is*," said Fitch; "but couldn't you tell us whether you are or aren't on one?"

"Suppose I said I wasn't here on a case—that I was here on a holiday to visit some friends—would you believe me?"

"I don't know," said Brenner.

"Well, there you are. I'm afraid there's nothing we can do about it. Now will you excuse me? As you can see, I have some friends waiting for me, and I'm anxious to get to my hotel."

"I'm sorry. I guess this wasn't the best time to try to talk to you," said Brenner. "You're staying at the Brevoort, aren't you?"

"Was that in the story, too?"

"Yes. Could I stop by in a couple of days and talk to you—not about whether you are or aren't here on a case

—but about Scotland Yard and police work in general?"

"Why don't you write me a note and we'll see?"

"Fair enough. Good morning." And he and Fitch went off, probably looking for the *Britannic*'s purser to see if there was anyone else on board that it was worth their while to interview.

"Journalists can be pretty useful, can't they?" said Sara as they walked up the dock behind the porter who was carrying Wyatt's bags.

"How?" asked Wyatt.

"By asking the questions you wanted to ask but weren't sure you should."

"Such as whether I was here on a case or not?"

"Yes."

"My answer to you is the same as it was to Brenner. Suppose I told you that I was here on a holiday. Would you believe me?"

"I'm not sure."

"Well, you've got the same problem he has—you don't know what to think. Now can we drop it?"

"Of course."

They got into a cab outside the pier, though, as Sara explained to Wyatt, Americans only called a two-wheeled hansom a cab. What they were riding in, called a growler or a four-wheeler at home, was called a coupé. And of course, if it was a four-wheeler with two horses, it was called a coach or a hack. Wyatt thanked her gravely for the information, then reminded her that he had been to America long before she had and stayed for well over a year.

"I knew that," said Sara undisturbed. "But I thought you might have forgotten." Then, as he grunted, "You're still upset about what happened at the dock, aren't you?"

"Do you blame me?"

"Well, it was a near thing, but after all it was an accident."

"Was it?"

"You mean it wasn't?"

"Let's not talk about it." He turned to Andrew. "How's your mother?"

"Fine. You'll see her. She said she'd wait and say hello before she left for the theatre."

"How is it going?"

"She says very well. She likes the director and the cast. And of course she likes the play. If she didn't, she wouldn't have come over."

The play was a dramatization of *Jane Eyre*, done by a British playwright who had been living in New York for the past few years. He had sent her the script saying that he thought that she was England's finest actress and that if she would agree to play Jane Eyre he would wait for years, if that were necessary, until she was free to do so. Verna knew flattery when she heard it, but she also knew a good script, and since she was more or less at liberty at the time, she decided to come over, bringing Andrew and Sara with her.

"I've nothing against the Brevoort," said Wyatt. "In fact, I like it. But I wondered why you're staying there instead of, say, the Hoffman House."

"Mother doesn't like big hotels," said Andrew. "She thinks the Brevoort has the best food in New York and besides it's very convenient to the theatre."

"Which theatre will she be playing at?"

"The Star."

"I don't believe I know it."

"It used to be the Wallack's," said Sara, "at Broadway and Thirteenth Street."

"Oh, of course. Wonderful theatre."

Since the Brevoort was at Eighth Street and Fifth Avenue, just a few blocks east of the White Star pier, it didn't take them long to get there. It was a low, white building with café tables in front of it, which made it seem particularly French. A porter came out to take Wyatt's bags and led the way up the few steps to the lobby. The desk clerk, Mr. McCann, was a friend of Sara and Andrew. He was fairly young, in his late twenties, and had worked with a carnival for a while. As a result, he had learned some sleight of hand and did simple magic tricks like making coins disappear or taking them out of the children's ears.

He greeted Wyatt respectfully, said he hoped he'd enjoy his stay in New York and, after he'd signed the register, gave him a note that had arrived for him a short while before. Wyatt thanked him and read the note as they followed the porter up the stairs to the first floor. This was another reason why Andrew's mother liked the Brevoort, Sara told him. Because there was no lift, or elevator as the Americans called it, and you could get your exercise running up and down stairs. The porter took them to Wyatt's room, which was next to the Tillett suite, overlooking Fifth Avenue and with a view of Washington Square and the Centennial Arch. Wyatt said it was fine and tipped the porter; then Andrew and Sara took him into the sitting room of their suite.

Verna, looking very attractive in a pale lawn dress, greeted Wyatt like the old and close friend that he was, embracing him and telling him how how glad she was to see him. Then, looking at him closely, she said, "Don't tell me something's happened *already*."

"What on earth do you mean?"

"I don't know. I thought you looked a little disturbed. And you must admit that things *do* have a way of happening when you're around."

"In London perhaps. But there's no reason why they should happen here."

"I hope not. Well, I'm off to the theatre. We're in the final stretch before the dress rehearsal. But you'll have dinner with us tonight, won't you?"

"Of course."

"Any plans for this afternoon?"

"I'm having lunch downtown with a friend."

Verna nodded. "You'll be able to take care of yourselves, won't you?" she said to Sara and Andrew. "You can have your lunch outside at the café."

"I thought I'd take them with me to meet my friend," said Wyatt.

"Oh? Well, I'm sure they'll enjoy that. See you this evening," she said and left.

"Was that what the note in your box was?" asked Sara. "An invitation to lunch?"

"Yes."

"And your friend won't mind if we come along?" said Andrew.

"I don't think so, but I don't care if he does."

"That's a funny thing to say," said Sara. "Just who is your friend anyway?"

"Inspector Sam Decker of the New York Police Department."

2

The Accident That Wasn't

When Sara and Andrew discovered that they were meeting Inspector Decker way downtown on Mulberry
Street, they urged Wyatt to go by El rather than take a
cab as he usually did when in London. They themselves
had fallen in love with the El when they had first arrived
in New York. Running high above the street on iron
trestles and going for miles, from the Battery on the south
to the open country of the Bronx on the north, the El—
short for Elevated Railway—offered some of the best,
most interesting and most varied views of New York
that it was possible to get. In places where there were
houses, the cars were so close to them that, while you
could not exactly reach out and touch them, you could
look into the windows and see how the people there lived
—what their kitchens and even their bedrooms were like.
And since the nationality of the neighborhoods changed

every few blocks—the Jews, the Irish, the Italians, the Germans, the Chinese all living in their own areas—a trip on the El was like a journey around the world.

It turned out that Wyatt liked the El as much as they did, so they walked over to Third Avenue, climbed the long flight of stairs to the El station, which looked like a transplanted Swiss chalet, and bought their tickets at an enclosed booth with a small wicket. The tickets were five cents each—which Sara and Andrew had learned to call a nickel. The ticket agent tore them off a large roll and pushed them out through the small opening. Wyatt took them and dropped them in the box as they went out on the long wooden platform. The train, three coaches drawn by the small, puffing steam locomotive, was already in sight up the tracks. It drew up at the station, the conductor opened the doors, they boarded it and were on their way downtown.

As they travelled south, the children told Wyatt about their schools. Though Verna had been anxious to have them come with her, she had been concerned about their missing even a few weeks of school. She had discovered, however, that she could place them at two separate schools: Andrew at a boys' preparatory school, and Sara at a so-called girls' finishing school. They were both closed now for the summer vacation, but during the time they had gone, both children had found them interesting, even though they were quite different from their schools in England.

"Different how?" asked Wyatt.

"Well, they don't do very much about European history," said Andrew. "Most of the boys in my class barely knew who the Stuarts were. On the other hand, I learned a great many things I never knew about, like the Sons of Liberty and the Boston Tea Party and the French and Indian War."

"And baseball," said Sara. "He's been playing baseball instead of cricket."

"And liking it?" said Wyatt.

"Yes," said Andrew. "It's a lot faster than cricket and great fun."

"What about your school?" Wyatt asked Sara.

"Very much the same as Andrew's. Except that we have a lot of elocution."

"You mean making speeches?"

"Either speaking or reciting."

"But why? Do they expect you to go into politics?"

"Of course not. It's not even for the theatre—which I'd like. It's all for society—which is what American girls go to school to be finished for. The teachers are always giving us Shakespeare on how,"—eyelids drooping, her tone became consciously dulcet,—" 'her voice was ever soft, gentle and low, an excellent thing in woman.' "

"Excellent indeed," said Wyatt gravely.

They got off at Grand Street and walked west to Mulberry. Police Headquarters was a four-story stone building with a green lamp on either side of the steps that led to to the large doors. They weren't going there, however. They were meeting Inspector Decker at an Italian restaurant diagonally across the street.

The restaurant was fairly crowded, but when they came in, a broad-shouldered man at a corner table got up and waved when he saw Wyatt, then looked startled when he saw Sara and Andrew.

"Hello, Sam," said Wyatt, going over to the table.

"It's been a long time, Peter," said the man shaking his hand and looking again at Sara and Andrew.

"Yes, it has," said Wyatt. "These are two young English friends of mine, Sara Wiggins and Andrew Tillett. Inspector Decker of the New York Police Department."

"It's very nice to meet you," said Decker with somewhat strained politeness. "I probably didn't make it clear in my note," he said to Wyatt, "that I wanted to talk to you."

"You made it very clear."

"But then I don't understand . . ." Again he glanced at Sara and Andrew, then looked more closely at Wyatt. "Are you annoyed about something?"

"Yes, I am."

"About what?"

"We'll go into it later. Right now I'm starving. I had breakfast at six o'clock."

"I'm sorry. Please sit down." He pulled out and held a chair for Sara, called over a plump, smiling man with a large mustachio, who was apparently the restaurant's owner, and had an animated exchange with him, partly in English and partly in Italian.

"Guido tells me that today's specialty is *osso buco*," he said. "I don't know if you know what that is. . . ."

"I know," said Wyatt. "We'll all have it."

"Your young friends too? Are you sure they'll like it?"

"Yes. They eat and like everything."

"Well, good for them," said Decker. He gave the order to Guido then, apparently trying to make amends and be a good host, he said to Andrew, "Tillett. Any relation to Verna Tillett?"

"She's my mother."

"Oh, well," said Decker, his face lighting up. "I saw her the last time she played in New York. It was a comedy at the Lyceum and it was one of the best performances I've ever seen in my life."

"It was probably one of Pinero's plays," said Andrew.

"It was. But the new one she's doing is a melodrama, isn't it?"

"Yes. A dramatization of *Jane Eyre*, opening in Boston in about two weeks."

"In Boston?"

"It will play there a week before it opens here."

"Well, I've got to see it when it comes here, wouldn't miss it for anything," said Decker. It turned out that he was not just an admirer of Andrew's mother, but a thoroughgoing theatre buff, and they talked about that—the theatre in London and New York—until their food arrived.

When Sara and Andrew tasted the *osso buco*—veal shanks cooked with wine and herbs—they nodded to one another, agreeing silently that once again Wyatt had introduced them to something delicious. Wyatt and Decker shared a bottle of wine. Then they all had *zabaglione*, a rich, custardy dessert, the two men had *espresso*, strong, black Italian coffee, and Sara and Andrew had *cappuchini*, coffee made with milk and topped with whipped cream.

"All right," said Decker, putting down his cup. "Now tell me what you're annoyed about."

"I'd like you to answer some questions first," said Wyatt. "Did you tell anyone I was coming here?"

"Well, yes," said Decker, a bit awkwardly. "As a matter of fact, I did."

"Who did you tell?"

"A reporter on the *World*."

"Did he do anything about it, say anything about it?"

"Yes," said Decker, even more awkwardly. "He wrote a column about it."

"Exactly what did he say?"

"He said . . . well, it's not going to make any sense unless I give you some background."

"Then pray do," said Wyatt coldly.

"Mark Twain once said, 'This is a great country. It

has some of the longest rivers in the world. And the rivers have more boats on them that travel faster and blow up more often and kill more people than anywhere else.' "

They all smiled politely.

"Well, there's something else that we've got, especially here in New York City. We've got more graft, bribery and general corruption than anywhere else since Sodom and Gomorrah. You've heard of Boss Tweed?"

They nodded.

"Well, he's gone, went to jail and died. And Dick Croker, another of the great political crooks, is gone, too. But the good work of robbing the public still goes on. The reason we know about it is that, besides having some good and honest men and some good and honest newspapers, New York City is usually run by the Democrats while the state legislature in Albany is usually Republican. And one of the ways the Republicans try to beat the Democrats is by launching investigations that will show just how crooked the Democrats are. Clear so far?"

"Yes," said Andrew who knew something about this and was following Decker with great interest.

"Well, about a year ago the state senate initiated an investigation to end all investigations. It was going to cover everything—the Police Department, the Water, Sanitation and Highway Departments—everything. The investigators opened an office just up the street here, almost opposite Police Headquarters, and from all reports they were really doing a job, coming up with things that no one had ever gotten before. Then, a few months ago, there was a fire and the office was gutted and all the material that had been collected was destroyed."

"Obviously an accidental fire," said Wyatt dryly.

"What a cynic you are," said Decker, smiling faintly. "And of course you're right. There wasn't much doubt but that it was arson; but there was no way of proving it or finding out who had done it. So the investigation was back to square one, and Albany had to decide whether to extend the life of the committee and start all over again or what. While they were arguing about it, something very odd happened. After the fire, quite a few of the men—not just politicians, but businessmen too —who had left the country supposedly for their 'health,' came back. And immediately after they did, some strange rumors started spreading—rumors that some of the targets of the investigation had been approached and told just how much it would cost them to keep their name clean and stay out of jail."

"In other words, someone had gotten hold of some of the material that the investigators had collected and was blackmailing them," said Wyatt.

"Exactly. What seems most likely is that before someone tossed in the torch, they stole one of the file cabinets, the one that had the most important evidence in it."

"But what's that got to do with me and what you told

the reporter from the *World*?"

"Well, as you probably guessed, they handed the whole mess to me. Though I'm a good Democrat, I don't like the way this city's being run and I haven't been afraid to say so. And so I've got this strange reputation of being an honest cop."

"Strange but deserved?"

"I'm afraid so. I wasn't brought up properly for the times in which we live and, as a result, I'll probably always be poor."

"Like many others."

"*Too* many others. Well, I started on the case right after the fire, almost four months ago. And while I have some strong suspicions, I haven't really gotten anything concrete. Everyone's been stonewalling me, refusing to tell me things I want to know, and I don't have the authority to make them talk. Then, a day or so after I got your letter saying you were coming, the reporter from the *World* came to see me as he'd been doing fairly regularly. He wanted to know how I was doing, whether I was getting anywhere. Of course I wasn't, but I didn't want to say so. Instead I told him that while there weren't any really new developments at the moment, there would be very very soon. When he asked why I expected them, I told him I couldn't say. But a minute or two later I said that you, a friend of mine from Scotland Yard, were coming over. He immediately put two and two together and asked if that was the new development I'd been talking about. I pretended to be upset and asked him why it should be, how that could have anything to do with the case. And he said what I thought he would."

"That detectives from Scotland Yard are the greatest in the world," said Wyatt ironically. "All geniuses."

"You're being sarcastic, but he did say something like that. But he said something else that was even more important. He said the reason I hadn't gotten anywhere and never would was that too many big men were involved. If I did come up with anything, I could be busted —either fired from the force or transferred out to the sticks. But no one could do anything, use any leverage, on an outsider like you."

"But why did you do it, put things in such a way that he'd come up with a ridiculous idea like that?"

Shamefaced, Decker shrugged. "I told you, I hadn't gotten anywhere, so I thought I'd stir things up a little."

"What do you mean?"

"I lived in upstate New York until I was sixteen. We were pretty poor and I used to do a lot of hunting—not for fun, but for food. Sometimes, when I was out without a dog, I'd walk through a field and I'd know there was game around even though I couldn't see any. So I'd throw a stick or stone into the bushes, and all of a sudden all sorts of things would break from cover."

"I see. And did your friend run the story in the *World*?"

"Yes. He said I'd gotten very angry when he'd suggested that you were coming over here to help me out on the case and that I'd denied it absolutely. But the way he wrote it left the impression that that's why you *were* coming."

Andrew realized now why he hadn't known anything about what Decker had told them. Verna got the *Times*, and though they knew that the *World* was a very good paper, they almost never saw it.

"And did anything happen as a result of the story?" asked Wyatt.

"No. I'm sorry to say, nothing did."

"Well, *I'm* sorry to say you're wrong," said Wyatt coldly. "Tell him what happened at the dock," he said to Andrew.

"The dock?"

"Yes. When you and Sara were coming to meet me."

"But that was an accident."

"Tell him!" repeated Wyatt firmly.

Andrew looked at him for a moment, puzzled, then recounted the incident, describing how the loaded cargo net had crashed down between them and Wyatt.

"But that's terrible!" said Decker. "No wonder you're upset. But after all, as Andrew said, it was an accident and—" Then, reacting to the grim expression on Wyatt's face. "Are you saying it *wasn't* an accident?"

Wyatt took a folded sheet of paper out of his pocket and handed it to him.

"I found this in my cabin when I went down to get my hat and coat, just before we docked."

Decker unfolded the note, read it and lost some of his color.

"What does it say?" said Andrew. "Can we see it?"

Decker glanced at Wyatt and, when he nodded, gave the note to Andrew. He and Sara read it together. It was written in a strong, decisive handwriting on good notepaper.

"We're warning you to keep your nose out of things that are none of your business," it said. "We mean this and we'll prove it." There was no signature.

"What you mean is, dropping that load of cargo was supposed to prove it," said Sara. "Prove that whoever wrote the note *did* mean business."

"So it would seem," said Wyatt.

"I'm sure that whoever did it didn't mean to hurt them," said Decker. "He probably didn't even see them, but . . . is that why you brought them along with you?"

"Since they had been endangered, I thought that was the least I could do. And since you were the one who, unintentionally, I know, put them in jeopardy, I thought you should meet them."

"Of course," said Decker. "And I'm sorry, very sorry. I apologize to you and to them."

"And will you be careful what you say about me in the future?" said Wyatt. "Make sure I'm not linked in any way with the case you just told us about or any other you're involved in?"

"Absolutely."

"What I can't understand," said Sara, "is who put the note in your cabin. Was it one of the crew?"

"No," said Wyatt. "Probably someone who came aboard with the pilot. Right?" he asked Decker, who nodded.

"But if that's so, couldn't you find out who it was?" asked Andrew.

"Probably," said Wyatt. "But I don't see the point. After all, I never was involved in this case of friend Decker's, and I'm sure that whoever sent me that warning note will soon realize it."

"I hope so," said Decker. He took out his watch and glanced at it. "I'm sorry, but I'm afraid I have to get back to headquarters," he said. He signalled to Guido and asked for the bill.

"No bill, Inspector," said Guido.

"Now wait a minute," said Decker. "You know I'm not that kind of cop. I don't accept free meals, don't accept any kind of gift."

"This not gift from me," said Guido. "Someone want you to be his guest, you and your friends."

"Who?"

Guido nodded toward a corner of the crowded restaurant. Looking that way, Sara and Andrew saw Dandy Dan Cady, the large and imposing man they had last seen at the dock. Sitting at the table with him was the thin man in the dark grey suit who had gotten off the ship just behind Wyatt. Decker, who had to turn to see who Guido meant, whistled softly.

"It's Dandy Dan Cady," he said.

"Who's that?" asked Wyatt.

"The big man in the Tenth, Eleventh and Twelfth Wards, probably the most important political boss in New York."

"I tell him okay?" said Guido.

Decker hesitated. "I don't like it," he said. "On the other hand, saying no is insulting, like refusing a drink in a bar."

"As I recall, men have been shot for that out west," said Wyatt, smiling.

"Well, I don't think that Dandy Dan would go that far," said Decker. "But there's no point in antagonizing him. All right, Guido. Thank him for us."

Guido nodded and hurried off. They all got up, and as they started for the door, Decker made a slight detour that took him close to Cady's table.

"Thank you very much, Dan," he said.

"My pleasure," said Cady, getting up. "I don't believe I know your friend," he said, looking at Wyatt.

"Inspector Peter Wyatt of the London Metropolitan Police."

"Oh yes. The man from Scotland Yard." He held out a carefully manicured hand. "Nice to meet you."

"Nice to meet you, sir," said Wyatt.

"And these are two friends of the Inspector's," said

Decker. "Sara Wiggins and Andrew Tillett."

"Hello," said Cady. Then, indicating the man in grey who was with him. "You know Biggsy, don't you?"

"Yes, of course," said Decker. "How are you, Biggsy?"

"Fine, Inspector," said the man in a quiet, rather cultured voice.

"That's good. Well, thanks again, Dan."

"Like I said, my pleasure," said Cady. "See you again sometime soon. And maybe I'll be seeing you again too, Inspector," he said to Wyatt.

"I hope so," said Wyatt politely.

"Who was that other man, Biggsy?" asked Andrew when they were outside.

"Si, short for Cyrus, Biggs," said Decker. "But everyone calls him Biggsy. He works with Cady, does all sorts of odd jobs for him. Why?"

Andrew glanced at Sara and she nodded.

"Cady was down at the dock when the Inspector's ship came in this morning," he said. "And Biggsy was *on* the ship, came down the gangplank right behind him."

Decker looked at him, then at Sara.

"Are you sure about that?"

"Yes," said Sara.

"That's interesting," said Wyatt. "But since I don't think their showing up here was any more an accident than what happened at the dock, it would be even more interesting to know how they knew where we were going to have lunch."

3

The Body in the Fountain

"Do you have any plans for this afternoon?" asked Verna.

It was shortly after lunch the following day, and they were in the sitting room of the suite, a large corner room with windows looking out on both Eighth Street and Fifth Avenue.

"No, we don't," said Andrew.

"I hope you don't intend to spend it indoors. It's much too nice a day."

"It's lovely," said Sara. "We were out all morning, over at the Farmer's Market on Gansevoort Street. We just thought we'd wait here for a while, keep you company till you went back to the theatre."

Verna, filing her nails, looked up. "Very thoughtful of you," she said. She glanced at Sara, then at Andrew. "Where's Peter today?"

"He's having lunch with someone, a chap who came over on the ship with him," said Andrew.

"And the reason you haven't made any plans is because you think he'll come back here afterward and take you somewhere."

"I wouldn't say we *think* that's what will happen," said Andrew. "But there's nothing wrong with *hoping* that he may want to do something with us, is there?"

"Yes, there is. You kept yourselves very busy before he got here, seeing school friends and going to all sorts of interesting places. But the minute he arrives. . . ."

"We just thought we should be around if he does want to do anything," said Sara. "After all, he is a visitor here."

"Ha, ha, ha," said Verna dryly. "I'll wager he knows New York a lot better than you do. You not only want to spend time with him because he's fun, but you're dying to find out about the case that brought him here."

"*Is* he here on a case?" asked Sara.

"Why, I assumed so. Isn't he?"

"We don't know," said Andrew. "We tried to get him to tell us, but he wouldn't."

"Very sensible of him," said Verna. "If he did, one way or another you'd try to get in on it, and I'm sure he's had enough of that, just as I have."

There was a polite knock at the door and Wyatt entered, followed by a sturdy young man in a corduroy suit, the man with the tawny beard that Sara and Andrew had seen with him just before he came down the gangplank.

"Good afternoon," said Wyatt to Verna. "I hoped you'd still be here. May I present someone who's been very anxious to meet you? Mark Russell, Verna Tillett."

Verna acknowledged the introduction with a smile and Russell bowed, though he had difficulty tearing his eyes away from her long enough to do so.

"And these are the two young friends I told you about, Sara Wiggins and Andrew Tillett."

"Hello," said Russell. "I believe I saw you down at the dock."

"That's right," said Sara.

"You came over on the *Britannic* with Peter?" said Verna.

"Yes, I did."

"I thought at first that you might be British like the rest of us, but you're American, aren't you?"

"Yes. A New Yorker, home after four years abroad."

"Travelling?"

"No, studying. Three years in Paris and one in London."

"Mark's an artist," said Wyatt. "I think a very good one."

"Where did you study in London? The Slade?"

"For a short while. But mostly with Walter Sickert."

"That's interesting. I know Sickert, was at his studio a few times."

"I know. That's where I saw you for the first time."

"I'm sorry. I'm afraid I don't remember it."

"I doubt if you saw me. You were just leaving. I asked Sickert who you were and he told me. We agreed that you were one of the most attractive and interesting-looking women in London."

"Sickert is a great flatterer, and I'm afraid you are, too."

"That's not true. One of his problems is that he's too honest and has made a great many enemies. Later on, of course, I saw you several times at the theatre. I thought your performance in *The Squire's Daughter* was one of the most moving I've ever seen."

"He told me that before he found out I knew you," said Wyatt. "When he discovered I did, he begged me to bring him here so he could meet you."

"I'm very glad you did. Will you be staying here now?"

"Yes. I've taken a studio on Twenty-Third Street, near the Art Students League."

"Perhaps Peter will take me there sometime. I'd like to see your paintings."

"I can't think of anything I'd like better. I brought quite a few things back from Europe with me, and as soon as they're unpacked. . . ."

"Perhaps over the weekend," said Wyatt. He turned to Sara and Andrew. "What have you two been up to?"

"We were over at the Gansvoort Market this morning," said Sara. "It was fun. There were farmers there from Long Island, New Jersey, even Connecticut. It reminded us of Covent Garden in London."

"It's very much like that," said Wyatt. "What are you doing this afternoon?"

"Nothing," said Andrew.

"Mark and I are going up to the Metropolitan Museum of Art. Would you like to come with us?"

"Oh, yes," said Sara. "We've been there several times, but we'd love to go again, especially with you and Mr. Russell."

"How does that sound to you, Mark?"

"What?" said Russell vaguely, glancing up, then down again.

"I've invited Sara and Andrew to come up to the Met with us this afternoon, and I asked if that was agreeable to you."

"Why, yes. Absolutely. Fine."

"Oh, my sainted aunt! You're not at it again, are you?"

"At what?" asked Verna.

"Sketching. He did it all the way over on the *Britannic*. We'd be in the smoking room talking—at least I'd be talking—and I'd suddenly realize he wasn't listening. He'd have that sketch pad of his in his lap and he'd be doing a quick sketch of someone on the other side of the room."

"That's what he's doing now," said Sara. "I wasn't

sure at first because he was keeping the pad hidden, but . . . were you doing Verna?"

"Of course not," said Russell, flushing. "I wasn't doing anything."

"Now, now," said Wyatt. "We're broadminded here and we'll put up with a great deal, but not with a fib. Let's see it."

"But it *isn't* a sketch. It's just some notes for what might be one, and—"

"May I see it?" asked Verna quietly. "I have a reason for asking."

"Why, yes. If you want to," said Russell, handing her a small notebook. "As I said, it's not even a sketch, but I couldn't resist trying to get *something* down—"

He broke off as she studied it. Sara, Andrew and Wyatt had moved around behind her and looked at it over her shoulder.

"I said that he was good," said Wyatt. "Do you agree?"

Verna nodded. And while Andrew did not consider himself an art expert, he could see why she did. With just a few lines on a sketch pad so small that it could be concealed in his hand, Russell had caught Verna; the proud and alert way she carried her head, the firmness of her chin, the warmth in her eyes and the hint of a smile in the corners of her mouth.

"I think it's top-hole!" said Sara. "A slap-up job."

"I agree," said Verna. She looked up at Russell, whose

face was now flushed, not with embarrassment, but with pleasure. "May I borrow this for a while?" she asked, holding up the notebook. "I'll get it back to you tomorrow."

"Of course. But why do you want it?"

"I'd like to show it to Ted Moss, our manager. He's been after me to go to Sarony and have him take a photograph of me that he can use in the lobby of the theatre, in advertisements and so on. But while Sarony's very good, everyone goes to him. I'd much rather have you do something—say a sketch to begin with and, if we have time, a portrait."

"There's nothing I'd like better!" said Russell, his face alight. "I work very fast. If you could give me, say, two or three sittings. . . ."

"That can easily be arranged," said Verna. "But first let me talk to Moss. I'm afraid I have to go now," she said, rising. "I hate being late for rehearsal."

"Can we drop you?" asked Wyatt. "We're going, too."

"Thanks, but there's no need for it. Though I could take a cab or even walk to the theatre, dear old Ted seems to feel that that's *infra dig* and insists on having a carriage call for me and bring me back here. Goodbye," she said, holding out her hand to Russell. "I'm delighted that Peter brought you here."

"I had a feeling that it was going to be a very good day when I woke up this morning," said Russell. "But I never dreamed it would be this splendid."

With a smile and a wave, Verna left. It took Sara only a moment to put on her hat, and they followed Verna downstairs and out to Fifth Avenue in time to see her being helped by a blue-jacketed coachman into a maroon coach with yellow wheels. He closed the door, mounted to the box and sent a spanking pair of bays trotting smartly up the avenue.

Wyatt started to signal to a hack but Sara and Andrew were able to persuade him to take one of the stage coaches that ran up Fifth Avenue. Drawn by two horses and with an open upper deck like the London buses, they were one of the best ways to see the city and, after the El, the young people's favorite means of transportation. Sara and Andrew sat in the front seats on the right hand side near the sidewalk with Wyatt and Russell sitting behind them. Russell had forgotten how impressive the mansions that lined Fifth Avenue were and commented on them, on the new hotels that bordered the plaza at Fifty-Ninth Street and remarked that the parade of carriages that entered Central Park at that point reminded him of Rotten Row in Hyde Park.

They got off at Eighty-First Street and crossed over to the huge and imposing building with its red brick and granite facade. Russell and Wyatt agreed that they would not try to characterize its architecture, which was not Gothic, Renaissance or Byzantine though it contained some elements of all of them.

They went up the wide stone steps and into the large central hall. Here Russell took charge and led them to the painting galleries where he pointed out and talked about the works he admired most, some of which had just been acquired but which he knew about because he'd seen them abroad or in art magazines. He showed them Manet's *Boy with a Sword* and *Woman with a Parrot*, the first two Manets ever to be bought by a museum. Though they spent some time in the Italian gallery, Russell's greatest enthusiasm was for the Goyas, the Renoirs and the Delacroixs. Andrew was pleased that he admired one of his—Andrew's—favorite paintings, Winslow Homer's *The Gulf Stream*. And though he approved of one of Sara's favorites, Rosa Bonheur's *The Horse Fair*, she was a little upset by his reaction to the one she liked best of all, Pierre Cot's *The Storm*, for he was unwilling to comment about it at first, and only when she pressed him did he say that he considered it a prime example of French academic art at its most insipid.

They had left the painting galleries and were on their way to the Greek and Roman collection when Russell saw a tall, scholarly-looking man walking toward the administrative offices.

"Ralph!" he called. "Ralph Holland!"

The man turned, peered at him through his pince-nez, then came over to them.

"But this is splendid, Mark! I didn't know you were in New York. When did you get back?"

"Just yesterday. I'd like you to meet some friends of mine." And he introduced Wyatt, Sara and Andrew to Holland who, it seemed, was the museum's curator of sculpture and antiquities and an old friend of Russell's. Holland was apparently very happy to meet them all, especially Wyatt, about whom he had heard from friends in London. He asked them what they thought of the museum and was pleased when Wyatt told him how much he liked it, comparing favorably with the British Museum.

"By the way," said Russell, "I understand that your Etruscan statues have finally arrived."

"Yes. They came in the day before yesterday and will be delivered here tomorrow morning."

"When will you be showing them?" asked Wyatt.

"The public showing will not be until next week. But we're having a private, unofficial viewing on Friday. You've probably read some of those ridiculous statements that there's something questionable about them. Well, to settle the matter once and for all, I've asked Alec Bowen Mowbray to come and look at them then."

"That should be interesting," said Wyatt. "I know Mowbray. I consulted him several times on art questions in London."

"Then perhaps you'd like to come to the viewing too —you, Mark and your two young friends."

"I'd like that. We all would."

"Good. See you on Friday at three o'clock, then."

And nodding to them, he went on toward his office.

"Who or what's an Etruscan?"asked Sara.

"A people who lived north and west of Rome between one thousand and five hundred B.C.," said Wyatt. Then, turning to Andrew, "Would our young scholar favor us with a well-known poem that concerns the Etruscans?"

" 'Lars Porsena of Clusium,' " said Andrew, striking a heroic attitude, " 'by the Nine Gods he swore that the great house of Tarquin should suffer wrong no more.' "

"I know that one," said Sara. "It's *Horatius at the Bridge*. I just didn't know that there were Etruscans in it."

"A very mysterious people," said Wyatt. "They crop up in all sorts of unexpected places."

"I really am anxious to see the statues," said Russell. "It's clever of George to have Mowbray look at them before they're shown officially. If he passes them, that will shut everyone up, even the Italians."

"Is he that much of an authority?" asked Andrew. "I always thought he was just an art dealer. I mean, he has a gallery in London, hasn't he?"

"And in Paris, and he's opened one here," said Russell. "But one of the reasons he does so well is that he *is* an authority. If he says a painting is a Giotto, it is. And if he says a statue is School of Donatello, it is. But the best thing about him is that he's becoming interested in contemporary art—and not just French painters, but Americans, too."

"Has he seen anything of yours?" asked Wyatt.

"No."

"Well, perhaps we can do something about that."

They stayed at the museum until closing time, then walked through the park to the Bethesda Fountain and along the Mall, where young children rode in small carts drawn by goats, a sight that had intrigued and delighted Sara and Andrew when they first arrived in New York. Early in the afternoon Wyatt had discovered that Verna was to be out for dinner that evening and, though he and Russell were going out to the theatre later to see John Drew and Ada Rehan in *The Taming of the Shrew*, he invited Sara and Andrew to have dinner with them first. Coming out of the park at Fifty-Ninth Street, he hailed a hack and told the driver to take them to Luchow's on Fourteenth Street.

One of the many things that Sara and Andrew had found fascinating about New York was the fact that each part of the city had a different national character. The area around Mulberry Street, for instance, where they had had lunch with Sam Decker, was Italian. But just south of it, on the other side of Canal Street, was Chinatown, where the signs in the shops were written in fascinating ideographs, while to the east the area was almost entirely Jewish. The German section was in Yorkville, in the east Eighties, though the most famous German restaurant in New York was Luchow's on Fourteenth Street.

Sara and Andrew had never been there before, but they found that it was just what they had imagined it would be: large and cavernous with boar and stag heads on the dark, oak-panelled walls. Large mirrors reflected the light of the ornate chandeliers and even the skylights were not of ordinary glass but had designs etched on them.

On Russell's recommendation they had sauerbraten and red cabbage, with apple pancakes for dessert, and though they enjoyed the dinner, it was so much heavier than what they were used to, they were glad to have an opportunity to walk a bit afterward.

They thanked Wyatt and Russell for the afternoon and the dinner, told Russell they hoped they would see him again soon, and walked west on Fourteenth Street to Fifth Avenue and then down to the hotel.

Their friend, Jim McCann, was at the desk.

"Did either of you lose a quarter?" he asked.

"I don't know," said Andrew. "Where did you find it?"

"Here," said McCann, taking it out of Sara's ear.

They laughed as they always did when he did one of his tricks.

"Any messages?" asked Sara.

"Not for either of you or Miss Tillett, but there is

42

one for Mr. Wyatt."

"He won't be back until quite late," said Andrew.

"Maybe we should take it upstairs and put it in his room," said Sara.

"No matter what time he gets back, there'll be someone here," said McCann. "But just as you like." And taking an envelope out of Wyatt's box, he gave it to Andrew.

"I wonder who it's from?" said Sara as they started up the stairs.

"It could be anybody."

"Not really. How many people know that he's staying here at the Brevoort?"

"If the reporter who said he was coming to New York put that in his article—and he must have because the *Times* man knew it—then anyone who read the *World* would know it."

"May I see the envelope?" asked Sara.

Andrew gave it to her, and they stopped under one of the gaslights in the corridor and examined it together. The envelope was ordinary and not very clean and the handwriting that addressed it to Mr. P. Wyatt was scratchy and irregular.

"It's certainly not from Inspector Decker," said Sara.

"Or from a university don. It's from someone who doesn't find writing easy and took great pains to make it legible."

"It's not sealed," said Sara, turning it over.

"Let's see," said Andrew. Then, examining it, "I think it *was* sealed, but the paste wasn't very good and when it dried it didn't hold."

"You know what I think? I think we should open it and read what's in it."

"Why?"

"Well, if it's not important it's not going to matter whether we read it or not. And if it *is* important, we know where to reach Peter. We can get him at the theatre."

"I always did admire your logic. Somehow it always justifies what you want to do."

"Does that mean you agree with me or not?"

"It means that I know better than to argue with you. Of course we'll tell him that we read the note."

"Of course," said Sara opening the envelope and taking out the single sheet of paper that it contained. The message on it, in the same hand as the address, was quite short.

"If it's worth a hundred bucks to you to find out who burned the investigation office and copped the file," it said, "meet me at the fountain in Washington Square at midnight tonight. Be sure and bring the money."

It was unsigned.

"Well," said Sara, "I'd say it was important."

"Why? Peter's not interested in all that. He's said so several times."

"Do you remember what he said to those reporters

and to us about whether he'd come over here on a case or not?"

" 'If I told you I *wasn't* here on a case, would you believe me?' "

"That's right. Well, I'm sure he *is* here on one."

"This one?"

"I don't know. Decker's his friend and in spite of what he said he may want to help him out. Or else it may be something very different. But I think he should have a chance to follow this up if he wants to."

"Maybe. But I don't think we have to go to the theatre for him. He should be back by midnight."

"Probably. We put it in his room then?"

"Yes. I'll push it under his door."

He put the note back in the envelope as they went on down the corridor. When they reached Wyatt's room, he pushed the envelope under the door, leaving one corner partly out.

"Don't you want to push it in all the way?" asked Sara.

"No. This way he'll be more likely to see it. And if we want to know if he's back later on, we'll be able to tell."

Sara looked at him approvingly. "Good," she said.

They sat in the sitting room of the suite for a while playing checkers, then went to their bedrooms. Andrew took off his shoes, but did not get into his pajamas. He stretched out on his bed and began to read Stevenson's

New Arabian Nights. At some point he must have fallen asleep, for, when he woke up with a start and looked at his watch—a repeater his mother had given him for his birthday—it was twenty of twelve. Putting his shoes back on, he crossed the sitting room to his mother's room and tapped softly on the door. When there was no answer, he opened it and looked in. It was empty. As he closed it, the door of Sara's room opened and she came out. Like Andrew, she was fully dressed.

"She's not there, is she?" she said.

"No."

"I didn't think so. I didn't hear her come home. I wonder if Peter's back."

"It's easy enough to find out."

They went out into the corridor. The corner of the note was still sticking out under the edge of the door.

"I guess he's not back yet," said Sara.

"No."

They looked at one another and each of them knew what the other was thinking, for they had both been thinking the same thing since they had read the note.

"If he's not back in a couple of minutes, he won't be able to meet whoever wrote the note," said Sara.

"No."

"And I think he would like to, don't you?"

"Yes."

"Then don't you think perhaps we'd better go out there and tell whoever it is that he's a bit late but that he'll meet him later?"

"It's what you planned all along, isn't it?" said Andrew, grinning.

"I wouldn't say I planned it. How could I when we both thought he'd be back by now? But I did think that if he wasn't. . . ."

"Right. Let's go."

They went downstairs and paused just before they reached the lobby. Jim McCann had gone off duty and the night clerk, a man they did not really know, was just going into the office behind the desk. Walking quietly but quickly, they crossed the lobby, went out and down the few steps to Fifth Avenue. A hansom went by, going up toward Fourteenth Street. But though there was laughter and the sound of voices coming from the Brevoort Café, the streets were deserted.

Keeping to the shadows near the buildings, they walked south toward Washington Square. The fountain was in the center of the square, about halfway between the marble Washington Arch and the rather Spanish-looking Judson Memorial Church. They did not approach it directly, but circled around to the east, toward the Gothic facade of New York University, and approached it from that direction. Though it was a fairly dark night, the gaslights set here and there in the park gave enough light to see the fountain clearly, even see the spray that jetted up from its center. And there was no one there, either standing there or sitting on the stone

47

curb that surrounded the fountain.

They paused behind the statue of Garibaldi, who stood drawing his sword just across the roadway from the fountain.

"What time is it now?" whispered Sara.

Andrew pressed the button on his repeater, and it began its faint, silvery chiming. When it had chimed five times, a church clock somewhere near them began striking the hour.

"It's just midnight," said Andrew.

"He's late."

"Yes. Let's give him a few more minutes."

They waited there, watching a lady and gentleman come out of one of the beautiful red brick houses on the north side of the square, get into a waiting carriage and drive off.

"Maybe he's on the other side of the fountain," said Sara finally.

"I doubt it. We'd see him."

"Not necessarily. Not where the water's shooting up."

"Do you want to walk around and see?"

"Yes."

"All right."

Coming out from behind the statue, they crossed the roadway to the fountain, started around it.

"Well," said Andrew when they were opposite the church, "are you satisfied? I told you he wasn't there."

48

"Yes. And I guess—" She clutched his arm. "Andrew, look!"

He turned, looking where she was looking, and there, floating face down in the softly splashing water of the fountain, was a man's body.

4

Benny the Monk

Though Washington Square had once been a potter's field, it later became quite fashionable. Some of New York's most distinguished families lived in the red brick buildings on the north side of it, which was probably why Sara and Andrew had so little trouble finding a policeman. For, like London and most other large cities, it was the neighborhoods where the wealthiest and best connected citizens lived that were most carefully patrolled. The two young people had barely convinced themselves that they were not imagining things and there really was a body in the fountain when they heard slow, heavy footsteps and saw a policeman, wearing a helmet very much like a London bobbie's, walking west on Fourth Street.

They ran over to him. Busy swinging his night stick— no, not swinging it; making it dance and pinwheel at the end of its leather thong—he did not notice them until they were in front of him. He started, listened skeptically to what they had to say, and then walked over to the fountain.

"Holy jumping Moses!" he said, then beat a rapid tattoo on the pavement with the end of his club. Apparently this was an established means of communication, because almost at once they heard an answering rapping from somewhere over on West Third Street, and a few minutes later another policeman came running down Broadway toward them.

"What is it, Joe?" he called. Then, as the first policeman jerked his head at the fountain. "Saints above! Dead?"

"Well, now does he look like he was taking a midnight swim?"

"Who found him?"

"The kids here." Then turning to them, "What are you doing out here anyway?"

"Meeting someone," said Sara. "At least . . ."

"At this time of night?"

"Yes."

"Where do you live?"

"The Hotel Brevoort," said Andrew.

The policeman looked at him, at Sara, and reassured by their appearance, said to his partner, "You stay here and keep your eye on the corpus. I'll walk them to the hotel, then go on to the station house and report it."

"You don't have to walk us to the hotel," said Sara.

"Yes, I do. I've got four of me own at home, and I wouldn't want any of them traipsing around by themselves at this hour. Besides, it's on me way." Then as they started across the park toward Fifth Avenue, "Are you British or something?"

"Yes," said Andrew.

"Well, I was born in Cork, but I've been here long enough to lose most of me justifiable prejudices. What are your names and how long have you been here?"

They told him and managed to answer his questions without having to tell him any of the things they preferred not to—such as who they were meeting and why —until they reached the hotel. They were afraid that he might go in with them, which would be awkward, but as they paused under the canopy, a hansom drew up and Wyatt got out.

"Well, what's this?" he asked, looking from them to the policeman.

"Was this who you went out to meet?" asked the policeman.

"Not exactly," said Sara evasively.

"My name's Wyatt. I'm a friend of theirs and of young Tillett's mother and I'm staying here at the Brevoort, too. Now can you tell me what this is all about?"

"They were out in Washington Square Park, and they found a body in the fountain there."

"A body?" He stiffened, looking sharply at Andrew who returned his glance with significant intensity.

"There was a note for you," he said. "But since you weren't here, we went out to take care of it."

"I see," said Wyatt, reading him correctly and understanding that there were things he did not want to say. "Do you know Inspector Sam Decker?" he asked the policeman.

"I know who he is, sir."

"Well, will you get word to him that Peter Wyatt thinks he should know about the body in the fountain and that I also think he should stop by here tomorrow morning and talk to me and my friends here."

It's unlikely that the policeman knew who Wyatt was, but he would have known he was someone of consequence even if he hadn't mentioned Decker's name.

"I'll do that, sir," he said, saluting. "Good night to you. And to the two of you," he said to Sara and Andrew and went off up Eighth Street toward the station house.

"Where's the note?" asked Wyatt.

"Upstairs, under your door," said Sara.

"Let's go up." He got his key at the desk, led the way upstairs, opened the door and picked up the note.

"How did it get up here?" he asked.

"We brought it up," said Sara. "Jim McCann said there was a note for you, and we thought it might be important."

"I assume you also read it," he said, reading it himself.

"Yes," said Andrew. "The envelope was open, and we

thought if it *was* important, we could get word to you at the theatre. But when we saw the time, we thought we wouldn't have to. That you'd be back by then."

"But when I wasn't, you thought you'd go meet the anonymous informant yourselves."

"That's right," said Sara. "Do you think he was the man who was killed?"

"How do you know he was killed?"

"Well, as the policeman said, it's not likely he was taking a midnight swim."

"No. But that doesn't mean either that he was the man who wrote the note or that he was killed. It's possible that he died of natural causes and—"

"Well, well," said Verna, appearing at the top of the stairs. "Am I interrupting something?"

"No," said Andrew. "Not really."

"Then could you tell me what's going on? I'm not inflexible about your bedtime, but even you will admit that this is a bit late for the two of you, unless there's some special reason for it."

"There is a reason for it," said Wyatt. "I don't know whether it's a good one or not, but . . . let's go inside, and we'll tell you about it."

They went into the sitting room of the suite, and taking off the shawl she wore over her ivory silk dress, Verna sat down and listened while Sara and Andrew told her what had happened, just as they had told Wyatt.

"Does this have anything to do with one of your

cases?" she asked Wyatt.

"No, it doesn't."

"Then who sent you that note and why?"

"I think I can tell you why if not who, but I'd rather not. I've asked a friend of mine, Inspector Decker of the New York City Police, to come here tomorrow. I think he should be told about the note and how Sara and Andrew got involved, and I suspect he'll be able to answer many of our questions as well as yours. So, especially since it's so late, why don't we hold them all in abeyance?"

"That sounds sensible," said Verna. Then, looking at Sara and Andrew with a frown that was only partly in jest, "As for you two. . . ."

"Yes, mother," said Andrew, and he and Sara both kissed her and went off to their respective rooms and beds.

Decker came to the hotel at a little after eleven the next morning. Sara and Andrew were in the sitting room with Verna at the time. She was going to Mark Russell's studio for her first sitting that afternoon—as a matter of fact, they were all going—and they were discussing what she should wear for the portrait when Wyatt brought Decker in. Though he was a fairly sophisticated man, his reaction was one that Andrew and Sara were used to, especially from men who had seen Verna on the stage. He did not stare, stammer and become much too courtly as some men did, but he did seem to find it hard to tear his eyes away from her and get to a discussion of the facts that was the supposed purpose of his visit.

"Yes," he said in answer to a question from Wyatt. "We've been able to identify the fellow in the fountain. He was generally known as Benny the Monk."

"The appellation, Monk, I suspect, was not used in its religious sense."

"No. It seems to have been short for monkey. If you had a chance to look at him, you'd know why."

"What did he do?" asked Andrew. "Was he a criminal?"

"It's hard to say. He was never booked for anything major—just vagrancy and drunkenness—but he hung around with known criminals, especially two who were suspected arsonists."

"Then he could have had something to do with setting fire to the investigators' office," said Sara. "Was he killed?"

"Just a second," said Decker. "Why do you connect him with the fire in the investigators' office? And what were the two of you doing out there at the fountain anyway?"

Sara and Andrew looked at Wyatt and when he nodded, they told the inspector about the note—which Wyatt gave to him—and then went on with everything that had happened after that.

"I see," said Decker thoughtfully. "To answer your question," he said to Sara, "yes, he was killed. With his history, we thought at first that he might have fallen into the fountain while drunk and drowned. But our surgeon said no. There was a wound on the back of his head. He'd apparently been hit there—that's what killed him—and then thrown into the fountain."

"That means that someone must have known about the note," said Andrew, "and killed him to keep him from talking."

"That's the way it looks," said Decker.

"May I ask a question?" said Verna. "Is this the case that brought you to New York?" she asked Wyatt.

"No, it's not. It's something I have absolutely nothing to do with."

Andrew tried to catch Sara's eye. For the first time Wyatt had not equivocated about whether he had or had not come to New York on a case. Which meant that he *was* on one.

"Then why did that Benny the Monk send you that note?" asked Verna.

"Tell her, Sam," said Wyatt. And somewhat awkwardly, Decker did so, not going into all the details, but covering all the important ones and especially the story about Wyatt that had appeared in the *World*.

"I see," said Verna. "I'm sure you know why I'm interested."

"Of course," said Decker. "You're worried about Sara and Andrew. While it was nothing that anyone could have foreseen, I'm sorry about what happened last night and I can't see any reason why they should have anything more to do with the case—or any other case—from now on."

"Good," said Verna, ignoring the young people's disappointed looks. "You've relieved my mind considerably. And now that we've straightened that out, would you like to have lunch with us?"

Though it was obvious that Decker would have liked to, he pleaded press of work and left. The four of them had lunch in the Brevoort restaurant, and a little before two they left for Russell's studio.

As the theatre was being readied for the dress rehearsal, which was to take place the next afternoon, there was no rehearsal that day. Nevertheless the carriage was at Verna's disposal, and they used that to go to Russell's studio. Andrew was the last one in, sitting on the outside with his back to the coachman. As he got in, he noticed a man standing near the hotel entrance, staring at them. He was in his thirties, powerfully built, and wore rather rough clothes: corduroy trousers and a short jacket over a checked shirt. He made no effort to avoid Andrew's eye, and as the carriage moved off, Andrew saw him step out into the street and hail a hansom.

Russell's studio was on Twenty-Third Street, a short distance east of Fourth Avenue and the National Academy of Design, a striking building that was by no means to everyone's taste, for it was built of marble and blue stone and was modelled after the Doge's Palace in Ven-

ice. The studio, on the other hand, was in an unpre-
tentious brownstone with a street-level entrance. As
Andrew helped Sara and Verna out of the carriage, a
hansom drew up a short distance beyond them and the
man in the checked shirt got out. Again he made no
effort to avoid Andrew's eye, seemed in fact to be seek-
ing it out. He paid off the cabby, then as Andrew hung
back, letting Verna, Sara and Wyatt walk ahead of him
toward the building, he came up to him.

"Got a nickel for a cup of coffee, mister?" he said.
The contradiction—calling Andrew mister and asking for
a nickel when he had just gotten out of a cab—were too
pointed to be accidental.

"I think so," said Andrew. He took out a nickel,
handed it to the man and felt something pressed into his
palm.

"Thanks," said the man, then he turned and walked
away. Andrew watched him go, then went after Verna,
Sara and Wyatt. What the man had given him was a
note, folded small. But since, in spite of his seeming
openness, the man had passed it to him secretly, Andrew
did not look at it then, but put it in his pocket.

Russell's studio was on the second floor, in the rear.
Wyatt, who had been there before, directed them to it,
knocked and then stood aside when Russell opened the
door. He was wearing a white shirt with the collar open
and the sleeves rolled up, and he greeted them warmly
as they walked in.

The studio was large and high ceilinged, with a big north window. Since Russell had leased it from a friend who had gone to Maine for the summer, it was furnished with a sofa, several low tables and comfortable chairs. A stack of paintings leaned against the wall in one corner of the room, and on a shelf above the wainscot that ran around the room were plaster casts of Greek and Roman heads.

Russell showed them the small bedroom and the kitchen and then, when they returned to the studio, he looked closely at Verna for the first time and broke off in the middle of a sentence. After her discussion with Sara and Andrew, Verna had decided that, since the portrait that Russell was doing was to be used in the theatre lobby and in advertisements, she should wear one of the costumes she wore in the play. The one she had picked was the one she wore when she first met Mr. Rochester on the road near Thornfield Hall; a black bombazine dress, black merino cloak and a black beaver bonnet, the only touch of color a cameo brooch that she wore at her throat.

"We never discussed what I should wear," Verna began, a little tentatively.

"No, we didn't, but we didn't have to," said Russell. "What you're wearing is perfect, exactly right! The black will bring out your coloring, which is wonderful, and the cameo brooch will give us just the note of contrast we need. I couldn't have done better if I'd thought about it for weeks. And now, if the rest of you will excuse us, can we get started?"

"Of course," said Verna.

He led her to the low platform in front of the window, sat her in a rather shabby armchair and then stepped back behind the easel he had set up to the side of the platform.

"Would you turn your head just a little to the left?" he said. "Just a little more. There. That's fine. Hold it for just a minute and then you can relax, talk, do anything you like."

He had a prepared canvas on the easel. Picking up a stick of charcoal, he began roughing in her face with sure, quick strokes. Sara, Andrew and Wyatt had seated themselves on the other side of the studio. They watched for a few minutes, admiring Russell's skill and assurance. Then Andrew took out the note that the man in the checked shirt had given him and unfolded it. While not exactly Spencerian, the handwriting was better than that in Benny the Monk's note to Wyatt. Andrew had a feeling—perhaps because of the unevenness of the letters—that it had been written in the hansom while the man in the checked shirt was following them.

"If you want to know what I think you do," it said, "write down where and when we can meet on the back of this and leave it for me. I'll be waiting to pick it up when you leave."

Sara glanced sideways at him. "What's that?" she asked.

Leaning close to her, Andrew told her and gave her the note. She read it, looked at him, then at Wyatt, mutely asking Andrew if she could give the note to the Inspector. Andrew nodded, and Sara touched Wyatt on the arm, whispered in his ear and gave him the note.

Wyatt read it, then looked thoughtfully across the studio. Andrew was fairly sure he knew what he was thinking. Decker had apologized to Verna for what had happened the night before in Washington Square—not that it was his fault that Sara and Andrew had gone out there—and Wyatt was trying to decide whether this note concerned that case or something else. Perhaps the case, whatever it was, that had brought him from England. More important, there was the question of whether there was any danger involved, not for himself, but for Sara and Andrew. Finally he made up his mind.

"What time is your dress rehearsal tomorrow?" he asked Verna.

"Two o'clock."

"How long will it last?"

"Probably until about five. Why?"

"I want to make an appointment and I wasn't sure what time to make it."

"Five thirty would be safe."

Nodding, Wyatt took out a pencil, wrote something

on the back of the note, folded it up again and gave it to Andrew, who put it back in his pocket.

"You're going to the rehearsal?" said Russell.

"Yes. We're all going," said Wyatt.

"Would you like to come too?" said Verna. "Or would you rather wait till we come back from the Boston try-out and open officially?"

"I already have tickets for the opening," said Russell. "But I'd like very much to come to the dress rehearsal too. It would give me a chance to make some sketches, which I won't be able to do on opening night."

"I'll leave your name at the door," said Verna.

"That would be very nice," he said somewhat abstractedly. He had put down the charcoal, picked up his palette and was studying Verna, then looking down as he mixed his colors. When he had what he wanted, he began laying the pigment on the canvas, starting with her face and painting as surely and quickly as he had when he was doing the rough charcoal drawing.

It was the first time Sara and Andrew had ever seen an artist at work, and they watched with great interest. After about ten minutes, Wyatt got up and walked to the corner of the studio where the canvases leaned against the wall.

"Are these yours?" he asked.

"Some of them," said Russell, continuing with his painting. "The ones on the outside. The rest are Thompson's, the chap I rented the studio from."

"May we look at them?"

"If you like."

"I'd like to see them, too," said Verna. "Bring them over here."

One by one, Wyatt brought the paintings over and set them up so that Verna could look at them at the same time that he, Sara and Andrew did. They were quite different from the kind of paintings that Andrew was used to; they were vivid in color and very strong. Yet with all their vividness and strength, much was left to the imagination. It was as if Russell was giving his *impression* of what he was painting rather than trying to reproduce it as a camera might. For instance, there was one painting of the Thames on a foggy day in which it was almost impossible to tell where the fog ended and the water began. And still it caught the essence of the river at such a time perfectly.

"Do you like them?" Andrew asked Sara quietly.

"Yes. Very much."

"So do I."

They stayed at the studio until a little after five. About four thirty, Russell looked at Verna and, though he himself seemed as full of energy as ever, decided that she'd had enough and made her get up and stretch. He made tea for them, which he served with some cakes from a local bakery, and talked very straightforwardly about his painting, what he'd done that he liked and where he thought he had not been completely successful.

Russell told Verna that he felt he'd made a good start on the portrait and would work on the background until she got back from Boston. He told Wyatt, Sara and Andrew that he'd see them at the dress rehearsal the next day, and then they left.

Verna had dismissed the carriage, and it took Wyatt a few minutes to flag a hack. While they waited, Andrew saw the man in the checked shirt standing in a doorway across the street. When they had come out of Russell's building, Andrew had lagged behind and, holding the door open, had ostentatiously pushed one corner of the note that Wyatt had returned to him into the slot of Russell's letter box, leaving the rest of it sticking out. As they got into the hack, Andrew saw the man with the checked shirt start across the street toward Russell's house.

5

Manion

Workmen were busy in the theatre lobby when Sara, Andrew and Wyatt arrived, touching up the gilt in the ceiling decorations and polishing the pendants of the chandeliers. Mr. Moss, the manager (whom Andrew and Sara had learned the Americans call "the producer"), was there watching and talking to Frank Talbot, the playwright. Andrew and Sara had met them both before and introduced Wyatt to them. Mark Russell got there a few minutes after they did, and they introduced him also. Moss told Russell how much he had liked the sketch Verna had shown him, asked how the portrait was coming along and then, looking at his watch, suggested that they go in.

The rehearsal started promptly, just a few minutes after two. Verna had told them that, on the whole, the Americans mounted their plays more lavishly than the

British, feeling that an elaborate production made the play seem better than it was. But even then they were surprised by the number of sets, the detail in them and the quality of the lighting.

What Talbot had done in his dramatization of the novel was to drop all the scenes of Jane Eyre's childhood and begin the action with her arrival at Thornfield. Thus Verna made her entrance just a moment or two after the rise of the curtain, and, as always, Andrew marvelled at her magic, her ability to become the character she was playing; in this case, the quiet but courageous governess. Sara stiffened a little when Jane Eyre met Adele, the young girl she was to take care of, and Andrew knew that it was because she wished she were up there on the stage playing the part. He squeezed her hand, and she smiled at him and relaxed.

Verna had originally become interested in the play because of the way the playwright had handled Rochester's mad wife, not using her for pure Gothic horror, but showing a certain amount of sympathy for her. She pointed out that while in this case the madwoman in the attic was real, it was still a symbol of much that went on in middle and upper class society. For if a woman was not free to develop and exercise her talents—and how many were?—then she, like Rochester's wife, was a prisoner in her own home. She made some suggestions as to how one section of the play could be rewritten—the scene in the attic in which Jane meets the wife—and the result was not just dramatic, but very moving.

There was no way that the book's famous line—Reader, I married him!—could be used in the play, but it did end very much as the book did, with that strong and difficult man, Rochester—now blind—breaking down when he discovers that Jane, whom he thought he had lost, has come back, and she takes him in her arms to comfort him as earlier she had comforted Adele.

The audience sat in silence for a moment after the curtain came down. Then, though there were only a handful of them—Sara, Andrew, Wyatt, Russell, Mr. Moss, the director, the playwright and a few others— they broke into a storm of applause and clapped even louder when the curtain went up and first the entire cast came forward to the footlights, and then Verna alone.

"Now, now," she said. "That's enough. You know you're all prejudiced."

"Of course we are, my dear," said Mr. Moss. "That's why we're stopping now and coming backstage. But I can assure you that the audience, which will not be prejudiced, will continue clapping until you're tired of taking curtain calls."

He rose and led them all backstage to the green room where Verna and the leading members of the cast were waiting. Verna had exacted a promise from Andrew a long time ago that he would always be honest with her about her performances. "Praise is easy to come by," she had said. "Honesty isn't. And if I can't get it from my own son, where can I get it?" It was a great responsibility for someone his age, but he tried to discharge it faithfully. And so Verna's eyes went to him first. And when he nodded, she relaxed a little. And when Sara and Wyatt nodded also, she smiled, embraced the two young people and was able to accept the congratulations of the manager, the director and the playwright.

They talked for several minutes, the other players coming in for their share of compliments, then Moss said he had some things to say to the cast about the performance and about the Boston trip. The director too had some directions for the cast and asked the visitors to excuse them. So the four left together, standing outside in front of the theatre and continuing to talk about the play and what they liked about it. Then, after reminding them that they were invited to the private viewing of the Etruscan statues at the Metropolitan Museum the next day, Russell went off to his studio, leaving the three of them alone.

"Ten of five," said Wyatt, taking out his watch and glancing at it. "Your mother's guess as to how long the rehearsal would take was a good one," he said to Andrew.

"You made the appointment for five thirty?"

"Yes."

"Where?" asked Sara.

"My room at the hotel. And since we've plenty of time, let's walk."

Their friend, Jim McCann, was at the desk when they got to the hotel. He greeted them, gave them their keys and gave Andrew some letters that had arrived for his mother.

"Who do you suppose the man is?" Sara asked when they were in Wyatt's room. "And what do you suppose he's going to tell us?"

"I've no idea," said Wyatt.

"You must have *some* idea."

"I haven't. Why should I speculate about it when I have quite a few other things on my mind? When he comes here—*if* he comes—he'll tell us, and that will be that."

"But . . ." began Sara, then broke off when Andrew nudged her. He didn't want too much discussion because he was afraid Wyatt might make them leave, even though it was he that the man had given the note to.

At about twenty of six there was a knock on the door and the man came in. He was not dressed quite the way he had been the day before. For though he was still wearing corduroy trousers, probably as a concession to this visit, he now had on a suit jacket and a proper shirt and tie instead of the checked shirt.

"My name's Manion," he said in a rather hoarse voice. "Al Manion."

"How do you do, Mr. Manion," said Wyatt. "Since you wanted to see us, I gather you know who we are."

"I know who *you* are. Your name's Wyatt and you're

English, from Scotland Yard. But I don't know who the youngsters are—except that they're friends of yours."

"Yes, they are. This is Sara Wiggins. And this is Andrew Tillett."

Manion nodded to them, then turned back to Wyatt. "Seeing how you're a 'tec and the British ones are supposed to be the best, you've probably figured out who I am and why I'm here."

Wyatt sighed. "I was asked to do that, guess who you were and what this was about, just before you got here. And I refused. But if you insist. . . ." He studied Manion's ruddy face, rough hands and the shoes that went with the trousers, for they were heavy and rather scuffed workshoes. "You do physical, outdoor work of some kind," he said. "I suspect something to do with ships."

Manion blinked. "Hey, that's pretty good! I'm a longshoreman, run a donkey engine for a stevedoring firm. But how'd you figure that out?"

"Your general appearance, but particularly your shoes. The white on the sides and soles looks like salt. You must have stepped in or been splashed with seawater and it dried there. But besides that, there are some tar stains on the bottoms of your trousers."

Manion glanced down. "Seems simple when you tell me, but it's still pretty good. And since you got that much, do you want to guess the rest—why I'm here?"

"Does it have anything to do with what happened the other day when I landed here on the *Britannic* and that cargo sling came down and almost hit me?"

"You got it. I was on the forward donkey engine at the time."

"And it was an accident?" asked Andrew.

"No."

"No?" said Sara. "You mean you did it on purpose?"

"Yes."

"But why?"

"Because I was paid to do it."

"By whom?"

"Before I get to that, I want to tell you that I never saw the two of you. I got kids of my own, and if I *had* seen you, thought there was even a chance of hurting you, I'd never have done it."

"I believe you," said Wyatt. "Now who paid you to do it?"

"You don't want to try to guess that?"

"No."

"All right. It was Dandy Dan Cady. He's not the one who made the arrangements and slipped me the dough. His buddy, Biggsy, did that. But it was for Dandy Dan."

"I see," said Wyatt. "I rather suspected that from some things my young friends here told me. Did Biggs give you any reason for it, say why he wanted you to do it?"

"Yes. He said you were coming here to stick your nose into something that was none of your business and Dandy Dan wanted to warn you to butt out. So he'd give me a signal when you came down the gangplank, and I was to drop a load of cargo as close to you as I could without really smashing you."

"I suspected that, too. But why are you telling us that now?"

"Why?" said Manion, his face darkening. "Because they crossed me up, that's why! I told Biggsy that doing something like that could get me into trouble, and he told me not to worry. That Dandy Dan would take care of it for me. Well, the stevedore boss not only fired me—he put out the word so that no one else'll hire me. And when I went to see Biggsy about it, he said he didn't know what I was talking about and that if I said anything about it to anyone, he'd really put the boots to me!"

" 'Don't tread on me,' " said Wyatt, nodding.

"What?"

"Wasn't that the motto on one of your early flags—that and a rattlesnake?"

"I don't know. But that's the idea. I don't take pushing around for anyone!"

"But still, you were rather careful about the way you got in touch with us," said Andrew. "The way you gave me that note for instance."

"Because whether I like it or not—whether I'm mad at him or not—Dandy Dan is one of the biggest men in this town. And while I want to get back at him, I'm not exactly anxious to have him know it."

"And you think the way to get back at him is through

me, is that it?" said Wyatt.

"That's right. If you've come over here to dig into something that he doesn't want you to—"

"I don't know how many people are laboring under that misapprehension," said Wyatt. "More than I like to think of. But I hope you're the last."

"What do you mean?"

"I didn't come over here to dig into anything that concerns Dandy Dan Cady. As a matter of fact, I never even heard of him until I got here. So if you're counting on me to even your score with him, I'm afraid you're in for a disappointment."

6

The Etruscan Treasure

Verna left for Boston the next morning. There had been
some discussion as to whether Andrew and Sara should
go up there with her. But since she was certain to be
very busy for at least several days, it was decided—much
to the young people's relief—that it would be best if they
stayed in New York where Wyatt could keep an eye on
them. Then, if all was going well, perhaps the three of
them could go up to Boston for the weekend.

The doorman had a hack waiting for them when they
came out of the hotel after lunch, and they had the
driver stop at Twenty-Third Street to pick up Mark
Russell, then went on again up to the Metropolitan Museum. Russell had received a note from his friend, the
curator, reminding him of the private viewing and telling
him where it was to take place. And so, instead of going
in the main entrance, Russell took them to the small,

75

ground-floor entrance. A uniformed guard just inside the door asked their names, checked them off on a list, and then turned them over to another guard who led them past the staff offices into a large hall that was empty except for a plaster cast of one of the friezes of the Parthenon and some Roman statues.

Russell's friend, Holland, was there. He was clearly having difficulty restraining his excitement, but he greeted them all warmly, introduced them to some of the other invited guests: the art critics of the *New York Times* and the *World* and several of the museum's trustees and their wives. The hall they were in, he explained, was intended for large-scale industrial exhibits. The Etruscan statues were in a small special exhibition room at the far end of the hall.

"Mowbray's not here yet, is he?" asked Russell, looking around.

"No," said Holland, frowning. "I don't know what's happened to him. I told him we'd like to begin at two thirty promptly, and . . ." He glanced at his watch, "here it is twenty of three. What do you think we should do?"

"Don't wait for him," said Wyatt.

"You don't think we should?"

"No. He always comes late because he likes to make an entrance. I think he'd prefer it if you went ahead."

"In that case, I think we will," said Holland, somewhat relieved. "We do have some quite important people here.

Ladies and gentlemen," he said, raising his voice, "will you come this way?"

He walked to the door at the far end of the hall, opened it, then stood aside while the invited guests filed in. Andrew was not sure what he expected to see, but when Sara, who was standing next to him, gasped, he knew exactly how she felt.

On a platform in the center of the room was the statue of a warrior that was at least eight feel tall. Wearing a breastplate, greaves and a crested helmet, he stood with his shield raised, brandishing a spear. The statue was made of painted terra cotta and, though the colors were somewhat faded, they were still vivid enough to give the statue special vitality. The dark, white-rimmed eyes glared from the round openings in the helmet, and the lips were clamped into a grim line.

There were two other artifacts in the room: a man's head, also larger than life size—possibly a priest since he wore an elaborate headdress—and a smaller, woman's head, her hair held in by an embroidered band, smiling a cryptic smile. These were both interesting, but inevitably everyone's attention came back to the giant statue on the central platform, which dominated the room.

There was a buzz of talk, exclamations of surprise and admiration, and then a spontaneous burst of applause. Pleased, but accepting it as his due, Holland bowed and smiled. He was about to say something when there were footsteps in the large hall and they heard a man's voice that seemed to be expostulating. Everyone turned to look at the open door, and in walked a very striking man, followed by a younger man and a museum guard. The man in the lead was in his early forties and, while of no more than average height, because of his manner and the way he carried himself, he was almost as imposing as the Etruscan warrior. When Andrew and Sara had first seen Dandy Dan Cady, they had felt that there was something extreme and self-conscious about the way he was dressed. But while this man wore a morning coat and striped trousers too, everything about him was relaxed and seemed exactly right. He wore a glossy top hat, tipped well back, and carried a silver-headed cane. A slim, blond young man, dressed as formally as he was, walked a step or two behind him and hurrying after them was a museum guard who seemed very agitated about something.

"Please, sir," he was saying. "Your stick!"

The man with the top hat—unquestionably Alec Bowen Mowbray—finally deigned to notice him. He paused and turned.

"What about my stick?"

"They're not permitted in the museum. May I have it, please?"

"What?" Mowbray looked at him in astonishment. "But if I give you my stick how can I poke holes in all the paintings?"

His mouth open, the guard looked at Mowbray and

then at Holland. The curator laughed feebly, then said, "It's all right, James," to the guard.

"Yes, sir," said the guard retreating.

"I'm delighted that you could make it, Mr. Mowbray," said Holland.

"I told you I would, didn't I?" He looked coolly around, and his expression did not change until he saw Wyatt. "Oh, Wyatt. Didn't realize you were in the States. How long have you been here?"

"About a week."

"Good show! Come and see me at the gallery."

"I'll do that."

"Splendid." Now, at last, Mowbray turned his attention to the artifacts. "These your Etruscans?"

"Yes. What do you think of them?"

Taking a monocle from his waistcoat pocket, Mowbray put it in his right eye, studied the warrior, walked completely around it, glancing at the man's and woman's head in passing, then paused, leaning on his stick.

"What do you think they are?" he asked.

"Think? I know what they are! They're sixth century B.C."

"Provenance?"

"Orvieto. They were dug up at Chiusi, the old Clusium."

"Who sold them to you?"

"Why, Bernardi. We only buy from the most reputable dealers. I asked you what you think of them."

"I heard you." Suddenly lifting his stick, he placed it under the giant warrior's raised right arm and pushed. The statue swayed, teetered, then as everyone gasped in horror, it crashed to the floor, smashing into a dozen pieces.

One of the trustees swore, his wife shrieked, and for a moment Holland stared, his mouth open in shocked incredulity.

"Merciful heavens, Mr. Mowbray," he finally whispered. "Why did you do that?"

"Because it's a fake," said Mowbray.

"What did you say?"

"I said it's a fake."

"But that's ridiculous, impossible!"

Russell had moved closer to the shattered statue and was looking down.

"No, it's not, Ralph. I think he may be right."

"Why do you say that?"

"Well, it's your field, not mine, but it's my impression that terra cotta statues were always cast in sections and then cemented together, so they didn't need an armature. But this one does have an armature."

"It may have needed one because it was so big."

Russell shook his head. "I doubt it," he said. He bent down closer to the metal skeleton that had been inside the statue. "Besides, this looks like steel rather than iron, and. . . ." He glanced up at Mowbray. "Could I borrow your glass, sir?"

Without changing his expression, Mowbray opened

his eye wide. As the monocle fell from it, he caught it and held it out to Russell.

"Thank you." Again Russell bent down, using the monocle as a magnifying glass through which he studied the metal framework. "Look at this. This rod is stamped Torino—Turin—and of course Turin didn't exist in the sixth century B.C."

"Oh." Holland looked at Mowbray as Russell returned his monocle with a bow. "What about the other two heads?"

"They're fakes too."

"Are you sure?"

"My dear fellow!" said Mowbray with infinite weariness.

"All right. All right. If you say. . . ."

"What are you going to do with them?"

"The two heads? Nothing. The museum can't show fakes."

"I can—if they're clearly labeled as such. As a matter of fact, I think it's amusing. I'll give you five hundred dollars for the two of them."

"Done!"

"Good. Roger," he said to the young man who had accompanied him, "give Mr. Holland a check and make arrangements to have them sent to the gallery." Glancing around at the assembled guests, he nodded to Wyatt. Then, swinging his stick, he walked out of the room, across the large hall and out of the museum.

7

The African Stars

They were having lunch the next day—Sara, Andrew and Wyatt—sitting at a corner table in the Brevoort dining room when Inspector Decker appeared at the entrance, looked around and then came over.

"I thought I might find you here," he said.

"One usually can," said Wyatt. "Join us?"

"I've had lunch, but I'll have some coffee," said Decker, sitting.

Wyatt signalled their waiter, ordered a *café filtre*, then said, "All right. Tell us."

"Tell you what?"

"I don't know, but you seem pleased about something."

"Pleased? Well, after the way things have been going with me it's made me feel a little better to learn that Scotland Yard isn't infallible."

Wyatt sighed. *"Et tu, Brute?"*

"Who else has kidded you about it?"

"Sara and Andrew are the only two other members of the genus homo sapiens that I've talked to so far this morning. And while as loyal and law-abiding Britons they did not, as you put it, kid me about it, they gave me the *New York Times* with as much interest as reticence and distress."

"You've seen it then?"

"The *Times*? Yes, of course."

"How much of the story is true?"

"The *Times* is your paper, not ours."

"I know. And it's usually quite accurate. But I couldn't help wondering. For instance—" he took the paper out of his jacket pocket, opened it to the story that was captioned *Lloyd's Settles Jewel Robbery Claim*—"it says here that it was one of the largest settlements they ever made. True?"

"Lloyd's has an office here. I imagine the *Times* checked with them."

"Probably. They paid out a hundred thousand pounds. That's about five hundred thousand bucks, isn't it?"

"Yes."

"What I don't get is why Lloyd's is so nasty about the Yard. I mean, things get stolen and sometimes you get the thief and sometimes you don't. If you don't, the insurance company pays up. But they seemed to imply that the Yard had a special responsibility here."

"We did have. Because we were supposed to be

watching the jewels at the time that they were stolen."

"How come?"

"It's a complicated story."

He glanced at Sara and Andrew as if asking permission to go over it again and they nodded, glad he was going to. For, when they had first read about it, it occurred to them that it was exactly the kind of case Wyatt might be involved in. Except, as Andrew had pointed out, it seemed to be all over since Lloyd's was paying up. And besides, neither of them could see how it could have brought Wyatt to New York.

"Do you know who Sir Harry Bachofer is?" Wyatt asked.

"Of course," said Decker. "He's the South African who owned the African Stars, the diamonds that were stolen, and is, I gather, rich."

"Yes. Except that you left out an adjective, the one that modifies rich. We usually say filthy."

"As in filthy rich? I thought that was understood. Even an averagely rich man doesn't ordinarily own three diamonds like that. Where did he get them, by the way?"

"From a mine that he found, developed and later sold. That, of course, is how he became so rich."

"And the Sir bit? How did he get to be a lord?"

"He's not a lord. He moved to London and a year or so after that he was knighted for 'services to the Crown.'"

"In the US that would mean he'd made a hefty contribution to the right political party."

"I'm afraid the same thing is true in England."

"How about the rest of the story—how the Yard got involved?"

"In gratitude for having been knighted, he gave the diamonds to the Crown. Not right away—they were to go to Her Majesty on her birthday. But since they were going to be Crown property, when Sir Harry and Lady Bachofer took the Stars to Italy to wear at the wedding of the Princess of Piedmont, Scotland Yard sent along a man to keep an eye on them."

"And is that where they were stolen, in Italy?"

"We don't know. The sergeant, a very reliable man, carried the diamonds from London, gave them to Lady Bachofer himself, accompanied her and Sir Harry to the wedding and the reception that followed, was given the diamonds afterwards by Sir Harry's valet and returned with them to London where they were put in a bank vault. The loss was only discovered a month later when Lady Bachofer decided to wear them one last time before they went to the Crown. The bank manager himself brought them to her. When the case was opened, it was found to contain a paste copy of the Stars—such a good copy that only an expert would have known it, but a copy all the same."

Decker whistled. "So there's no telling when they were stolen. You say the sergeant was a very reliable man. Did anyone else get near them?"

"Only Sir Harry's valet, who took them from Lady Bachofer and gave them to the sergeant. And if we thought the seregant was reliable, Sir Harry swore by the valet. He'd only been with him a year, but he'd been valet to the Duke of Denham for fourteen years before that. Naturally we talked to him and he told a very straight story. The poor fellow was so upset at what had happened that, shortly after he left the Yard, he walked in front of an omnibus, was run down and killed."

"Rough luck."

"Yes. And that, I think, is enough of that. Anything new on your case?"

"The missing file? No. That's why I selfishly said I was glad to hear that you people don't always come through. I've gotten absolutely nowhere with it—no new leads, nothing. I'm about ready to give up."

"There are cases like that—more than the public realizes. On the other hand—" He broke off as their waiter came to the table with a yellow envelope in his hand.

"A telegram for you, sir," he said.

"Oh, thank you." Wyatt ripped open the envelope, took out the message and read it. "Well, this in interesting."

"What is it?" asked Decker.

"It's from Daniel Cady."

"Dandy Dan?"

"Yes. And it says, 'Urgent that I see you as soon as

possible. Let me know where and when by return message.' "

"Well, well. Do you know what it's about?"

"I think so."

"Will you see him?" asked Sara.

"I suppose I should. And since he says it's urgent, I'm afraid we'll have to put off our trip to the Statue of Liberty," he said to the two young people.

"That's all right," said Andrew.

Wyatt beckoned to the Western Union messenger, a boy of about fourteen, who was waiting just outside the dining room. "Do you have a reply form?" he asked.

"Yes, sir," said the boy, taking a pad and pencil out of his pocket.

Wyatt thought a minute, wrote a note on the yellow form, folded it and gave it to him.

"What's the charge on that?" he asked.

"No charge," said the boy. "The sender will pay." Then when Wyatt tipped him. "Oh, thank you, sir. Thank you very much." And saluting, he hurried out of the dining room.

"When did you make it for?" asked Sara.

"An hour from now. Two thirty."

"He couldn't ask for anything sooner than that," said Decker, getting up. "I'll run along. I'm assuming you'll let me know if it's anything I should know."

"Of course," said Wyatt.

Cady must have been fairly close by and as anxious to see Wyatt as the telegram suggested, for at exactly two thirty, there was a knock at the door of Wyatt's room, and when he opened it, Cady came in, followed by his unobtrusive companion, Biggs.

"Afternoon, Inspector," he said. "It was good of you to—" He paused, staring at Sara and Andrew.

"You met my young friends, Sara Wiggins and Andrew Tillett, didn't you?"

"Yes, at Guido's. I'm a little surprised to find them here."

"Well, we *are* friends. And we had a date. We were going out to the Statue of Liberty. Have you ever been there?"

"No. Somehow New Yorkers never get around to seeing any of the sights tourists do. Well, I don't suppose it matters. I thought we should have a little talk."

" 'The time has come, the Walrus said, to talk of many things.' "

"What?"

"It's from *Alice in Wonderland*," said Biggs. "A children's book by a chap named Lewis Carroll."

"It's true that it's generally considered a children's book," said Wyatt. "But I've found that the older I get, the more I get out of it."

"I'm not much of a reader so I wouldn't know about that," said Cady. "All right if I sit down?"

"Please do."

"Thanks." Adjusting the crease in his trousers, he seated himself near the window. "I'm sure you know why I wanted to see you."

"Why should I know that?"

"I just think you do. Didn't you have a visitor the other day who talked to you about me?"

"Who was that?"

"I must say you play it pretty close to your vest," said Cady, smiling. "But that's all right. I'm talking about Al Manion."

"Yes. He was here, and he did talk about you."

"He told you that I was behind what happened down at the dock when you landed. That I arranged to have him scare you by dropping a slingful of cargo in front of you."

"He did say something like that. Is it true?"

"Yes, it is. That's one of the reasons I wanted to see you—to tell you how sorry I am about it. Particularly since the kids here might have gotten hurt. I didn't know —no one knew—that they'd be around and might be in danger. You believe me, don't you?" he said, turning to Sara and Andrew.

They exchanged glances and shrugged.

"Since you seem to be in a confessional mood," said Wyatt, "perhaps you'll tell me why you did it."

"I did tell you. To scare you off. There was a story in the *World* that you were coming over to help find one of the files that disappeared after the fire in the office of the state investigating committee. Is that true?"

"That that's why I was coming over here? Certainly not."

"But you do know about the file?"

"I've heard about it. You say that one of the reasons you came here was to apologize for what happened down at the dock. Was that because you knew we'd been told you were responsible?"

"Yes."

"In other words, you're admitting it because you know we already know."

"That's right."

"I must say you're being refreshingly honest." Then as Cady smiled, "What other reasons did you have for coming to see me?"

"As you probably gathered, I've changed my mind about a couple of things. It was stupid of me to try to scare you off. I should have known you wouldn't scare for two cents."

"That may or may not be true. But what's that got to do with anything? I told you I'm not the least bit interested in that precious file of yours. As a matter of fact, I didn't even know it existed until I came here."

"But now that you do know, how much would you want to find it for me?"

"What? Why do you want it found?"

"Oh, I always wanted it found. As a matter of fact, I've had my own detective working on it for some time now. I just didn't want *you* to find it."

"Because there's material incriminating to you in it?"

"Of course. I've been in politics for a long time and you can't stay in politics—in this town anyway—and stay as clean as a lily. But my man hasn't been able to find it, and the police haven't, and it's important that it *should* be found."

"Because whoever does have it has been using the material in it for blackmail?"

"Right. After thinking about it, I decided I'm not too worried about what they might have on me. I'll be able to handle it. But I am worried about what's happening to some of the really big men in this town—aldermen, contractors, even bankers. Whoever's got the file has been putting the squeeze on them, and they've been coming to me and crying about it, so what do you say? Will you take on the job of trying to find it?"

"What makes you think I could find it?"

"I just do. Detectives from Scotland Yard are supposed to be the best there is."

"Nice of you to say so, but we're not infallible. If you read the *Times* this morning you know that we got absolutely nowhere with the theft of the African Stars."

"So no one's perfect. But from what I hear, your average is pretty high."

"Thanks. But I'm afraid it's impossible."

"Why?"

"Inspectors of the London Metropolitan Police don't

take on private cases."

"Who'd know it?"

"I'd know it."

"That's silly. You're here on a holiday, aren't you? I've been asking around and no one in our police department knows of any case you're on, so . . . what if I said I'd pay you ten thousand dollars if you found that file for me?"

"I'd still say no."

"Twenty-five thousand?"

"Sorry," said Wyatt, smiling faintly and shaking his head.

"Hmm. Biggsy, looks as if we've got a real tough one here," said Cady, getting to his feet. "Well. . . ."

"May I ask you a question, Mr. Cady?" asked Sara.

"Of course, Sara. It is Sara, isn't it?"

"Yes. Did you have anything to do with what happened to Benny the Monk?"

"Who?"

"Benny the Monk."

"Who's he?"

"You'd know him if you saw him," said Biggs. "Small, rather funny-looking chap who used to hang around the club. He wasn't very reliable—used to drink quite a bit— but he was all right on small jobs, running errands and that sort of thing."

"Oh, yes. I think I remember him. But why do you ask about him? What did happen to him?"

"He's dead," said Sara. "Someone hit him on the head and threw him into the fountain in Washington Square."

"What?" Cady turned to his companion. "Did you know that?"

"Yes," said Biggs. "The police came around, wanting to know what I could tell them about him."

"What made you think I had anything to do with that?" Cady asked Sara.

"I just thought I'd ask," said Sara. "I was interested because Andrew and I were the ones who found him."

"Oh. Well, to answer your question, I didn't have anything to do with that. I've done a lot of things my grandmother might not approve of, but that's not the kind of thing I go in for."

Sara looked at him thoughtfully for a moment, then nodded, indicating that she believed him. And though Andrew had learned that chronic liars can be very plausible, he found himself believing Cady too. At least about this.

"It was nice to talk to you," said Cady, shaking hands with Wyatt, "even if I didn't get anywhere with you. Speaking of which, will you at least think about the proposition I made you?"

"I'll undoubtedly think about it because it was quite flattering," said Wyatt. "But I can assure you I won't change my mind about it."

"That's that then," said Cady and, nodding to Sara and Andrew, he went out followed by Biggs.

"Well, that was interesting," said Andrew when the door had closed.

"Quite," said Wyatt.

"What I'd like to know," said Sara, "is how he knew that Manion had been here to see you."

"The same way he knew we were going to be having lunch with Sam Decker," said Wyatt. "And where we were having it."

"You mean someone here told him?" said Sara. "Who?"

"I think I know," said Wyatt. "But if you want to make sure. . . ." He took out a notebook, wrote something in it, then tore out the page, folded it and gave it to Andrew. "Go out and walk over to Washington Square or along Eighth Street. Find a likely-looking boy —a newsboy or shoeshine boy—give him this note and a dime and tell him to deliver it to the desk here. Then hurry back yourself. Sara and I will be waiting on the stairs."

"Right," said Andrew. He glanced at the note as he went down the stairs. Wyatt had addressed it to himself. He waved to Jim McCann, the desk clerk, as he went by, nodded to the doorman outside and walked down Fifth Avenue to Washington Square where he found a newsboy and followed Wyatt's instructions. Then he hurried back to the hotel, going in the side entrance. He found Wyatt and Sara where Wyatt had said they would be: on the stairs where they could look into the lobby without being seen. Wyatt raised an inquiring eyebrow, and Andrew nodded. Then the newsboy came in, accompanied by the doorman, gave the note to McCann and went out again. McCann glanced at the note, and as he turned and put it in its proper box, Wyatt went down the stairs and over to the desk.

"Good afternoon," he said.

"Oh, good afternoon, Mr. Wyatt," said McCann, turning back again. For some reason he seemed a little awkward, uneasy.

"Anything for me?"

"Yes. As a matter of fact, something just came."

As he started to turn again, get the note in the box, Wyatt reached across the desk and took him by the arm.

"No," he said quietly. "Stay where you are."

"I beg your pardon?" said McCann, looking at him in surprise.

"I said, stay where you are. Andrew, will you nip in there behind the desk and bring me the note from my box?"

McCann went white. Andrew glanced at him, went around to the side of the desk where there was an opening, went in and took the note from the box and gave it to Wyatt. Wyatt unfolded it, and it was blank.

"But that's not the note you wrote," said Sara. "Where's that?"

"I suspect in Mr. McCann's sleeve," said Wyatt, releasing him. "Right, Mr. McCann?"

His face expressionless, McCann took a folded piece of

paper from inside the cuff of his sleeve and dropped it on the desk.

"But how?" said Sara. "Why?"

"It's a fairly old trick," said Wyatt, "sometimes used in theatres or carnivals as part of a supposed mind-reading act. In this case, the real note was palmed and a blank piece of paper was put in the box. Then, when our friend here had a chance to read and perhaps copy the real note, the blank paper was removed and the actual note put in its place. As to why he did it, you'll have to ask him that."

"It's because of my wife," said McCann in a husky, uncertain voice. "She's sick, in the hospital, and I needed money. Someone offered me a lot of it if I'd let him know about any messages you got. I didn't see that it would be doing any harm, so I said I would."

"Who was it?" asked Sara.

"Please don't ask me. That's another reason I had to do it. He's a very powerful man and if I told you who he was and he found out—"

"Never mind then," said Wyatt. "Don't tell us."

"What are you going to do?" asked McCann. "You'd be right if you went to the manager and told him about it. But if you did, I'd be fired and . . ."

"I've no intention of going to the manager about it," said Wyatt. "Just don't do it again."

"No, Mr. Wyatt. No, I won't. And thank you. Thank you very much."

They went back upstairs quietly, soberly.

"So that's how Cady knew you were having lunch with Sam Decker and where," said Sara.

"Yes."

"What did you write in this note?"

Wyatt handed it to her. She unfolded it and read:

"Just the place for a Snark! I have said it twice.
That alone should encourage the crew.
Just the place for a Snark! I have said it thrice.
What I tell you three times is true."

"That's not from *Alice in Wonderland* too is it?" asked Sara.

"No. It's by Lewis Carroll, but it's from something else, *The Hunting of the Snark*. For some reason it seemed appropriate."

8

The Real Treasure

They made their postponed trip to the Statue of Liberty the following morning. Walking across Eighth Street to Sixth Avenue they took the El down to South Ferry, chugging along high over the streets behind the small, puffing engine. There were four Elevated lines in Manhattan, running from the Battery on the south to the Harlem River on the north. And, of the four, Sara and Andrew liked the Sixth Avenue one best because its route lay almost exactly in the middle of the island, and when you rode on it, you could see the whole width of Manhattan from the coach windows, from the East River on the east to the Hudson on the west.

At the Battery they took the small boat out to Bedloe's Island, site of the statue, and there they had the misfortune to run into a guard whose father had come from Notting Hill, not far from where Sara had grown up, and who was so excited about meeting three real Britons that he insisted on following them about and telling them more about the statue than they wanted to know. For instance, he told them that its correct name was *Liberty Enlightening the World*. Executed by the French sculptor, Bartholdi, it was the largest statue made in modern times and is one hundred and fifty one feet high. He was just telling them about her arms, hand, and head, in which forty people can stand, when a large group of tourists approached him with some questions and the three were able to escape, hurrying into the base of the statue and up the stairs inside. Not content with the view from the head, they went up an even narrower stair to the chamber in the torch itself. Here, over three hundred feet above the water, the view, which took in Manhattan, Brooklyn, Staten Island, New Jersey and the Lower Bay, was really breathtaking.

The overfriendly guard was busy with a crying child, evidently separated from its parents, when they came down, and they waved their goodbye to him as they left the statue and walked over to get the boat back to Manhattan.

"Hungry?" asked Wyatt as they got off at the Battery.

"Yes," said Andrew.

"Anything special you'd like for lunch?"

"If I know you," said Sara, "you've already made up your mind about where we're going and what we're having."

"Is that so?"

"Yes. But I'm quite happy to leave it in your hands."

"In that case, let's make use of our *feet* first."

He led them over to South Street and north along the East River docks. They walked under the bows and—since there were almost as many sailing vessels as steamers here—sometimes under the bowsprits of ships from a dozen ports and with a hundred different destinations. It was while they went past the many piers that Andrew suddenly realized there was another way in which New York differed from London. Though the Thames runs through London and many ocean-going vessels make the trip up it and dock there, there are few streets in New York that don't end up in a river with access to the sea. He remembered *Moby Dick* by Herman Melville, who had died here in New York just the year before. It was a book he had liked enormously, and in it Melville had talked of "your insular city of the Manhattoes, belted round by wharfs as Indian isles by coral reefs." It was true. And it was also true that the Battery, which they had just left, "was washed by waves and cooled by breezes which a few hours earlier were out of sight of land."

He had further proof of just how much of a seaport New York was as they approached the towering suspension bridge that connected Manhattan and Brooklyn, one of the world's greatest engineering feats and one of the sights of New York. He sniffed, aware that Sara was sniffing too. Along with the salty smell of the sea there was another, stronger smell.

"Fish!" said Sara.

Smiling, Wyatt nodded. The large, green building with its gables and cupolas that stood at the river's edge and partially overhung it was the Fulton Fish Market, much like London's Billingsgate Market, he told them. Tied up at the piers behind it, they could see fishing schooners from all up and down the coast, discharging their cargoes of fish, lobster and shellfish.

He led them up a flight of stairs to a restaurant on the second floor of an old brick building. It was noisy and quite crowded; almost all the scrubbed wood tables were taken, but they managed to find a small one near the window that overlooked the cobbled street where carts and wagons were being loaded and moved off to the clatter of horses' hoofs and the grinding of iron rimmed wheels.

"Do you know what you want?" asked Wyatt.

"We'll leave that to you too," said Sara.

"We can't have oysters, unfortunately. They have more different kinds here than you've ever heard of, but they're not in season. However, we can have clams. Have you ever had chowder?"

"No," said Andrew.

"Three chowders," he said to the shirt-sleeved waiter who had appeared at his elbow, "and three lobsters."

The chowder arrived, steaming bowls of it thick with clams, potatoes, onions and tomatoes and seasoned with thyme. As they ate it, Wyatt told them of the continuing battle that raged between those who insisted the only legitimate chowder was New England chowder made with milk and those who liked Manhattan chowder, the kind they were having, made without milk but with tomatoes.

"I don't dare say this above a whisper," he said. "At least not here, but I've had both and they're both delicious."

Andrew and Sara agreed that the Manhattan chowder certainly was and made mental notes to try the New England version when they joined Verna up in Boston.

The lobsters were boiled, split and served with drawn butter and chips, which they had learned the Americans called French fried potatoes. And, loyal defenders of British sea food though they were, they had to admit that these lobsters were the best they had ever eaten, even better than the Cornish lobsters of Andrew's childhood. When they had finished, they were so full that they reluctantly refused any dessert, even the ice cream that the waiter assured them was homemade.

"Now what?" asked Sara when they were downstairs on South Street.

"Haven't you had enough of me and general activity?" asked Wyatt.

"Of course not," said Andrew. "But if you've had enough of us, say so."

"I haven't. But I do have an appointment a bit later on, at three o'clock."

"With anyone we know?" asked Andrew.

"Yes. Mark Russell. I'm taking him up to the Mowbray Galleries. I got in touch with Mowbray and he agreed to look at some of Mark's paintings, see if he'd be interested in giving him a show."

"Can't we come too?" asked Sara. "We like Mark Russell, and I also like Mr. Mowbray."

"Why?"

"I just do. I think perhaps because he's such a character, convinced that he's the greatest art expert there is."

"Which he probably is. All right. If you'd like to come along, you can."

And that's how it was that a few minutes before three they got out of a carriage at Thirty-Third Street and Fifth Avenue, Russell carrying several of his canvases and accompanied by Wyatt, Sara and Andrew.

The Mowbray Galleries, quite new, were in a handsome marble building. A uniformed doorman opened the carriage door for them and tried to take the canvases, but seemed to understand when Russell told him he'd rather carry them himself. The young woman at the desk inside asked their names and told them that Mr. Mowbray was upstairs in the gallery proper and was expecting them. They went up the stairs to the gallery, which was large and well-lighted with skylights as well as windows set high on the north wall.

Mowbray was in a small viewing room off the gallery with a client, a heavy, red-faced man smoking a large cigar. The two Etruscan heads, of the priest and of the woman, were on a stand just inside the door. Mowbray waved to Wyatt and gestured, indicating that he would be with them soon. Then, nodding to his young assistant, he said, "All right, Roger."

Roger picked up a canvas that was facing the wall, turned it and placed it carefully—even reverently—on an easel.

Mark Russell, standing near to Andrew, drew in his breath sharply and became very still, and Andrew knew why. It was a painting of a young woman—probably Dutch judging by her starched white headdress—sitting at a desk and writing a letter. It was one of the most beautiful paintings he had ever seen.

"This is the painting I told you about," said Mowbray. "The one I said I wanted you to see." He paused and stepped back, his eyes fixed on the painting. "Vermeer," he said. "Jan Vermeer of Delft. Painted in 1670 when he was at the height of his powers. As he usually did, he has shown his subject, a young woman, doing something quite ordinary—in this case, writing a letter. I call your attention to the light, Vermeer's chief characteristic. Many of the Dutch and Flemish painters were interested in light, but it was always golden sunlight. Vermeer was the only one who made use of this particular clear and silvery light—a light that gave his colors a completely different value from the colors of any other painter."

"Yes, I see," said the man with the cigar. "To tell you the truth, I was thinking of a different kind of painting."

"Were you?" said Mowbray with ominous restraint. "What kind?"

"Something a little more like. . . . Well, say the one in the Hoffman House bar." Leering, he sketched some voluptuous female curves with his cigar. "Know what I mean?"

"Yes," said Mowbray in arctic tones. "I know exactly what you mean." Though Andrew had never been to the Hoffman House bar, he knew what the man meant too. For when the painting—a large oil of a group of buxom, underclad nymphs playing with a satyr—was first hung it caused a sensation and had been reproduced many times since in newspapers and magazines. "Roger, will you show Mr. Stoessel out?"

"Now wait a minute," said the man with the cigar.

"I'm asking you to leave, you overblown, underbred philistine! Now will you go or shall I ask Roger, not to show you, but to *throw* you out?"

"You can't talk to me that way! Who do you think you are, anyway?"

"I know exactly who I am. I'm Alec Bowen Mowbray

and it seems that even I can make a mistake. I should have suspected that anyone who made his fortune in beef might prefer those blowsy cows at Hoffman House to a Vermeer. But, having recognized a mistake, I try to correct it. So, for the last time, will you leave here, sir?"

Glaring at Mowbray and muttering under his breath, the man with the cigar stumped out of the viewing room and down the stairs.

"Well," said Wyatt, "success has not changed you much. You're as gracious, temperate and amiable as ever."

Mowbray smiled faintly. "It's a luxury I permit myself. Can you imagine how I'd feel if I had actually sold this Vermeer to that porcine butcher?"

"It's beautiful," said Russell, his eyes on the painting. "As beautiful as the one at the Metropolitan."

"Yes, it is," said Mowbray.

"You've seen each other before," said Wyatt. "At the Met. But I didn't have a chance to introduce you then. Mark Russell. And two young friends of mine, Sara Wiggins and Andrew Tillett."

"How do you do?" said Mowbray, bowing to Sara and Andrew. "I remember the two of you. I take it you like my Vermeer?"

They nodded mutely.

"Good. And you needn't feel that you have to say anything about it. Most people's comments about art are absolute nonsense. As for you," he said, turning to Russell, "I remember you, too. It was you who noticed that the armature of that fake Etruscan statue was contemporary, made in Turin."

"Yes," said Russell. "But in point of fact, we've met before. At Whistler's studio in London."

"Ah, yes. You're a friend of his?"

"I'm afraid I can't say that, although I would like to. I admire his work tremendously."

"A very good painter," said Mowbray nodding. "But a difficult man. Almost as difficult as I am. I understand that you're a painter, too."

"Yes."

"Did you bring any of your things for me to look at?"

"Well, yes. But . . ."

"Let's see them."

Removing the Vermeer and leaning it against the wall, he gestured toward the easel. Russell untied the cord that held his paintings together and, somewhat hesitantly, picked one up and put it on the easel. It was the Thames scene that Andrew, Sara and Wyatt had seen at Russell's studio. Mowbray stepped back, studied it carefully for a moment, then nodded.

"Let me see another," he said.

Russell put a second painting on the easel, then a third.

"How many more do you have at your studio?" asked Mowbray.

"That I really like? I'd say five."

"That's eight. When you've done another seven or

eight, let me know and I'll come and look at them. If I like them as much as I like these, I'll give you a one-man show."

"Do you mean it?" said Russell.

"Of course, I mean it," said Mowbray testily. "I never say anything I don't mean. Your painting is strong and individual. You've studied the Impressionists, learned from them, but developed your own style. Like Eakins and Ryder, it's very American. And I like it." He turned to Wyatt. "I was quite sure if you said he was talented, I would agree. My compliments."

"Thank you," said Wyatt. "I haven't had a chance to tell you yet how much I admired your performance at the Metropolitan the other day."

"Oh, that," said Mowbray, glancing at the two heads on the stand. "A little melodramatic, I'm afraid."

"Perhaps. But effective."

"So it seems. I probably wouldn't have been able to convince Holland of the truth if I hadn't been a bit melodramatic. But I'm sure you've done the same thing in your cases when you wanted to make a point—done something rather extreme, I mean."

"Yes, I suppose I have. Never quite with your flair and panache. But after the example you gave me . . ."

Turning, he pushed first one and then the other of the Etruscan heads off the stand. They fell to the floor and, like the giant warrior, smashed to bits. Sara, Andrew and Russell stared at Wyatt, each of them, they admitted later, secretly fearing that he had taken leave of his senses. Then they looked down and stared again. For lying among the broken shards of terra cotta were three large and gleaming diamonds hanging as pendants from a silver chain.

Moving as quickly as Wyatt had, Mowbray stepped to the door of the viewing room, closed and locked it, then leaned against it.

"How did you know?" he asked quietly.

"I can't say I *knew*," said Wyatt. "I suspected—my suspicions beginning with something my friend Russell here told me."

"Just a second," said Russell. "What is all this? What are these?"

"I know," said Sara. "They're the African Stars."

"The diamonds that the *Times* wrote about the other day? The ones that were stolen from Lady Bachofer?"

"Yes," said Wyatt, picking them up and putting them in his pocket.

"And you said you guessed they were here because of something I said?"

"I said my suspicions were first aroused by something you said. You told me you'd run into a chap you'd known in Paris named Lamarre who told you that he was making a good living now faking old masters. That the last thing he'd done was a Rubens."

"Not true," said Mowbray. "I assume you talked to him, learned that he was working with Otto Getz and discovered a connection between Otto and me."

"Yes."

"No one asked Lamarre to *fake* a Rubens. He was asked if he could paint in the *style* of Rubens. When he said yes, I gave him the subject, went over his palette with him and gave him a lecture on Rubens brushwork."

"What happened to the picture?"

"It was sold as *school* of Rubens. When it was brought to me, I said that—while I found it very interesting—I could not possibly authenticate it, pointing out the ways in which it differed from known works of Rubens."

"But also pointing out ways in which it was similar."

"Yes. But go on. What made you think I had anything to do with the diamonds?"

"I was asked to look into the case by the Yard after they disappeared, did some investigating and discovered that you knew Sir Harry, had visited the Bachofer house several times."

"He wanted to buy some paintings," said Mowbray, nodding. "But his taste was execrable, as bad as that meat packer's, so I refused to sell him any."

"I also discovered that you had been in Rome at the same time as the Bachofers. That you had gone there about two weeks before and stayed a few days longer than they did. And while you were there you spent a good deal of time with Bernardi, who has often been suspected of dealing in questionable artifacts."

"But I don't understand," said Russell. "Why were they hidden in one of the Etruscan heads?"

"To get them out of Italy and to the United States," said Wyatt. "There was too much excitement about the theft to try to smuggle them out by the usual methods or to try to dispose of them there. Though I'm sure Bernardi wasn't aware of what you were up to."

"Certainly not or that would have been the end of them. I concealed them in the woman's head myself, packed in with plaster of Paris. What I did—as a favor to him, he thought—was to drop a few hints about a marvelous Etruscan find that I knew would get to Holland at the Met."

"But how were the diamonds actually stolen?" asked Andrew.

"It was the valet, wasn't it?" asked Wyatt.

"Yes," said Mowbray. "I'd given him the paste copies, and he substituted them when he gave the case to the sergeant to take back to London."

"But why did he do it?" asked Sara. "Inspector Wyatt said that Sir Harry trusted him completely. That he'd been with the Duke of Denham for fourteen years."

"That's right, my dear. And do you know what the duke left him when he died? Fifty pounds. Fifty pounds after fourteen years of service! And while Sir Harry thought it was quite a feather in his cap to have gotten him, the valet—Jeffries—couldn't stand Bachofer and knew it would only be a question of time before good old Sir Harry sensed it and gave him the sack. So it was easy to get him to agree to do what I wanted for a competence that would let him quit immediately and live comfortably for the rest of his life."

"But unfortunately he died almost immediately," said Wyatt.

"Yes, he did, poor fellow," said Mowbray. Then, looking sharply at Wyatt, "You don't think I had anything to do with his death, do you?"

"I wondered."

"Well, I didn't—I give you my word, I didn't. I think what happened was that he was so upset at everything that had been going on—what he'd done and being questioned by Scotland Yard—that he didn't look where he was going and walked in front of the omnibus."

"But why did *you* do it?" asked Andrew. "Steal the diamonds, I mean. After all—" He hesitated.

"After all, I seem to be a gentleman," said Mowbray, smiling. "I don't look or talk like a thief—whatever you think a thief looks or talks like. My answer couldn't be simpler. I needed the money."

"You?"

"That surprises you, does it? Well, it should. I'm the best known—and best—art dealer in the world. And probably the best art critic as well. But at that time I did need the money. I had a gallery in London, the one on Bond Street. But I wanted to open one in Paris and one here. Where was I going to get the money for that *and* for pictures to sell in all three galleries? Your friend, the Inspector here, told you about one thing I did—that so-called school of Rubens painting. But I didn't like doing it—even though it brought some money to a quite good artist also. So I decided to do something else."

"Steal the African Stars," said Sara.

"Yes, Sir Harry had been to my gallery and I'd met him at the homes of friends and I didn't like him. I thought it would be rather a lark to get the diamonds away from him. And I knew it wouldn't hurt him much since they were insured. So I worked out the details of the dodge."

"But why did you leave them—the diamonds, I mean—here in the gallery?" asked Andrew.

"Why not? Can you think of a safer place for them than inside a terra cotta head that I myself had called a fake? Besides, I rather liked the idea of keeping them here, keeping them handy. Because I was convinced that it was here, at the gallery, that I'd find the proper person to sell them to—someone with a great deal of money and few scruples who'd be willing to buy some extraordinary diamonds without inquiring too closely as to where they came from."

"But so far, I gather, no one with exactly those qualifications has turned up," said Wyatt.

"Yes, they have. I could have disposed of them at least twice. But would you like an example of pure and classic irony? Shortly after I arranged the theft of the diamonds

—and some time before they arrived in this country—I no longer needed the money. I made some very large sales—a Titian and a Raphael—and two different clients offered to lend me as much money as I needed to open the galleries here and in Paris. That's why I still have the diamonds."

"Don't you mean *had* them?" asked Wyatt.

"Well, yes. Which brings us to a most interesting question. What happens now?"

"Why, I go to the police, make my complaint, and they arrest you for grand larceny."

Smiling, Mowbray shook his head. "What a silly move that would be."

"Silly?"

"Yes. I would of course deny that I knew anything about the diamonds. I was as surprised as you were when you found them in the head. Obviously, my proclaiming the heads to be fakes and putting them in my gallery prevented the real thief from recovering his stolen goods."

"Even though I have witnesses to the fact that you admitted the theft?"

"Witnesses? What witnesses? Our friend Mr. Russell here—to whom I have promised a one-man show—a promise it would be difficult for me to keep if I were in jail? I have a feeling he might be rather reluctant to testify against me."

"What about us?" asked Sara. "Andrew and me?"

"I'm not sure how much weight the police would give to the testimony of two minors, especially friends of Inspector Wyatt's," said Mowbray. "Besides," and again he smiled, "I have the impression—perhaps erroneous—that you are not quite as outraged at what I did as you should be. That you rather like and, in fact, admire me and thus—even though the Inspector is your friend—like Mr. Russell you would prefer not to testify against me."

Wyatt looked thoughtfully at Sara and Andrew as they exchanged glances.

"May I ask you another question?" said Mowbray. "Why did you come to America?"

"To see if I could find the African Stars and return them to their rightful owners."

"Well, you've done that—found them, I mean. Isn't that enough for you? Do you need to go into every detail of how and where you found them?"

Wyatt studied him for a moment, glanced at Russell, Sara and Andrew, then looked at Mowbray again.

"Perhaps not," he said.

"Splendid," said Mowbray, unlocking and opening the door. "I was quite sure that anyone as clever as you are would also be reasonable. Which brings me to a final point. You recall," he said to Russell, "that I told you that I liked your work—thought you were very talented —*before* the Inspector played out his little melodrama. I meant it. And I meant it when I said I'd give you a one-man show."

"Yes, I know you did," said Russell. "Thank you."

"No, no," said Mowbray. "Thank you—all of you—for a most interesting and, in the end, most satisfying half hour."

9

The Midnight Caller

Mark Russell had dinner with Wyatt, Andrew and Sara that evening. And since both Russell and Wyatt had things to celebrate—Wyatt the recovery of the African Stars and Russell the promise of a show for his paintings —they went to Delmonico's. Of course Sara and Andrew knew about Delmonico's—it was New York's most famous and reputedly its best restaurant—but they had never been there before. Wyatt had booked a table for them in the café, which looked out on Broadway and Twenty-Sixth Street and was a little less formal than the dining room, which faced Fifth Avenue. The café was large and high-ceilinged with a marble floor, and the furnishings and general decor were most elegant. Russell followed the example of Sara and Andrew in asking Wyatt to order for them, and, after consultation with the waiter, he asked for Clams Casino—clams baked with

bits of bacon and herbs—mutton chops with baked potatoes, salad and strawberry ice cream for dessert.

They spent the early part of the evening talking about
Mowbray, whom, it turned out, Wyatt liked as much as
Russell, Sara and Andrew did—though he hastened to
point out that a great scoundrel is often much more interesting and amusing than someone of impeccable moral
character. They knew that the African Stars were now
in the hotel safe, and Wyatt intended to turn them over
to Lloyd's the next day for return to the Bachofers.

After dinner they started down Broadway together.
This section of it—from Thirty-Fourth Street down to
Fourteenth—was known as the Ladies' Mile, for it was
lined with some of New York's finest and most expen-
sive shops: jewelers, furriers, florists, milliners and shops
that sold only gloves. The street was full of coaches,
victorias, landaus and barouches even at this hour, and
the pavement was crowded with strollers for, besides the
shops, there were many theatres along this stretch of
Broadway.

When they reached Twenty-Third Street, they
paused, for Wyatt and Russell were going to Koster
and Bial's Concert Hall and, though Sara and Andrew
had hoped that they might be asked to come along, they
weren't—Wyatt explaining that after the performance
they were going to visit friends of Russell's and would
be home very late. Sara and Andrew didn't know why
they couldn't go to the theatre with them—though it was

called a concert hall, it was really a music hall with the kind of variety show that the Americans called vaudeville—and go home afterwards. But they didn't say anything about it. Instead they thanked Wyatt for a delicious dinner, said good night to Russell and walked over to Fifth Avenue and then downtown.

"Why so quiet?" asked Andrew after they had gone several blocks in silence.

"You know why."

"Because of what's going to happen now."

"Of course. Now that Peter's gotten what he came here for—the diamonds—he'll leave and go back to England."

"I don't think he'll go right away. He'll want to stay and see Mother's play open here in New York and that won't be for almost two weeks."

"I don't know about that. If he goes up to Boston with us this weekend, sees the performance there, he may not stay for the official opening here."

"I think he will. Didn't he say something about taking a holiday—that he hadn't had one in two years?"

"Yes. But how do you know he won't go back and take it in England?"

"Would you if you were he?"

"No. I'd take it here—at the Jersey shore or Newport or that place Mark Russell was talking about with the sand dunes and miles and miles of beach where the artists go."

"Provincetown on Cape Cod."

"Yes. But we'll see."

The night clerk was on duty when they got back to the Brevoort. He said good evening to them, looked in their box and told them there were no messages for them when he gave them their key. They said good night to him and went upstairs. The suite seemed very large and empty with Verna away and, after talking for only a few minutes in the sitting room, they each went to their own room.

Andrew had recently discovered Kipling and was now reading *Soldiers Three*. Becoming deeply involved in the exploits and adventures of the oddly assorted trio, he read until a little after eleven and fell asleep almost as soon as he had turned off the light.

He woke with a start, not sure what had awakened him. Then he heard it again, a soft but persistent tapping on the door of the suite. Picking up his watch, he saw by the glow of the streetlight outside that it was a quarter to twelve. He got out of bed and went into the sitting room just as Sara came out of her bedroom.

"Did you hear it?" she whispered.

"Yes."

"Who do you think it is?"

"I don't know." He went to the door. "Who is it?" he asked.

"Al Manion," said a husky voice.

Manion. The longshoreman who had come to tell

them why he had dropped that load of cargo near them on the dock. Andrew looked questioningly at Sara, and when she nodded, he opened the door a few inches and peered out. Having made certain that it was Manion—Andrew could see him clearly by the light in the corridor—he opened the door and let him in.

"Is anything wrong?" asked Sara.

"I'm looking for your friend, Wyatt. I've been knocking at the door of his room, but there's no answer."

"He's out," said Andrew.

"Any idea when he'll be back?"

"Late," said Sara. "He was going to the theatre and then out visiting."

"Rats!" said Manion impatiently. "There's not much time."

"For what?"

"I told you what Dandy Dan told me. That your friend was coming here to stick his nose into something that wasn't his business and Dandy Dan wanted him scared off. Well, I found out what that something is. It's a filing cabinet that a lot of people are looking for."

"Yes, we know about that," said Sara. "Do you know where it is?"

"I don't, but I know someone who does. The thing is, he's real nervy, anxious to get out of town. If I go back and tell him I couldn't reach your friend, he'll tell me to forget about it."

Again Andrew and Sara exchanged glances.

"Peter said that it had nothing to do with him," said Andrew. "That he wasn't the least bit interested in it."

"I know. But Inspector Decker is—very interested. And Peter's his friend, so wouldn't he want to help him?"

"I suppose he would."

There was something compelling, almost fateful, about this development. They had heard about the file cabinet the day Wyatt arrived and things had happened because, in spite of his denials, people had insisted on believing he was interested in it. And so it would be, not just satisfying, but poetic if he were able to help Decker recover it before he left.

But along with this there was something else—something Andrew knew Sara was thinking too—that here was another chance for them to do something on their own. And this time they might be more successful than they had been with Benny the Monk. He knew they shouldn't even be considering it, but it was hard to resist.

"Do you think this chap would talk to us, tell us where the file cabinet is?" he asked Manion.

"He might. If you like, I'll take you to him."

"Where is he?" asked Sara.

"Across town, at the East River."

Again Sara and Andrew looked at one another.

"Let's do it!" said Sara.

"All right," said Andrew. "Give us a couple of minutes to get dressed," he said to Manion.

"Sure. But don't you think maybe you should leave a note for your friend Wyatt, so that if he comes back before you do, he won't worry?"

"Good idea," said Andrew. Going to the desk near the window, he scribbled a short note on hotel stationery, put it in an envelope.

"Give it to me," said Manion, "and I'll shove it under his door."

"Fine." Andrew gave it to him, went into his room and dressed quickly. When he came out, Sara was just coming out of her room.

"Where's Manion?" she asked.

"Putting the note under Peter's door."

When they went out into the corridor, Manion was there, waiting for them.

"Ready? Good. Look, I'm still worried about Dandy Dan or someone else knowing I had something to do with this, so let's not go out through the lobby. I don't want the desk clerk to see us together."

"We can go down to the café and out that way," said Sara.

"That's what I thought," said Manion. "That's the way I came in."

They went down the stairs, past the lobby and out through the side door of the café onto East Eighth Street which, at this point, was called Clinton Place. They started walking east but they had only gone a short distance when a hack came up behind them. Manion hailed it, told the driver to take them to the Hunter's Point Ferry station, then followed Sara and Andrew in and closed the door.

"Is that where we're going—Hunter's Point?" asked Sara.

"No. But the chap we want is waiting near the ferry station."

Sara asked him who the man was, but he said, "You'll see," looking behind the hack as if he were afraid of being followed. He was so clearly uneasy that they didn't ask him any more questions. They went east on Eighth Street, past Avenues D and E, finally drawing up in front of the ferry station on the river. They got out, Manion paid the driver, and he drove off. The ferry was not in the slip, and there was no one in the ferry station. The whole area was deserted, silent except for the lapping of the water against the piles and bulkheads that edged the river.

Manion started walking north, and they went with him. Two blocks further on they saw their first sign of life. A steam launch was tied up at a dock. It was thirty-five or forty feet long, almost large enough to be called a yacht, and had a cabin with several portholes in it. Its running lights were lit and it had steam up—they could see a faint trail of smoke rising from the stubby stack and the glow of coals in the firebox as the engineer opened the door to look at the fire.

Another man stood at the edge of the dock. He was a

tall, powerful man with a flat face and snub nose wearing a peaked seaman's cap. He glanced at Sara and Andrew as Manion led them down toward him, but he didn't say anything.

"Is that the man?" asked Sara.

"No," said Manion. "On board."

He jumped down onto the open deck behind the cabin, helped Sara and Andrew down, then slid open the cabin door.

"In there."

Sara and Andrew went in. The cabin was low, with a table running down the center and lockers covered with cushions on both sides of it. An oil lamp hung from a hook overhead and by its light they could see that the cabin was empty.

Andrew turned, puzzled. "Where is he?" he said. "There's no one—"

Before he could finish the sentence, the cabin door was slammed shut and they heard a lock snap. At the same time, they heard the slap of wet ropes as the lines were cast off and the launch swung away from the dock and moved out into the river so suddenly and swiftly that they were almost jerked off their feet. A pair of innocents, they had walked into a trap and were being taken to someplace unknown with no idea of why or by whom.

IO

The Island

"Well, well," said Andrew.

"A fine pair of idiots we are!" said Sara.

"Egregious!"

"What's that mean?"

"From *ex*—out of. And *grex, gregis*—herd or flock. Meaning outstanding."

"That's us. And we thought we were so clever. At least, I did. The young detectives!"

"It wasn't just you. I thought so, too."

"Who do you think it is? That's copped us, I mean."

"I don't know."

"But Manion was in on it, wasn't he?"

"Of course. It was he who just locked the door. Though I think it's called a hatch. And I suspect he's still on board." He peered out through the forward porthole. "Yes. There he is talking to the big man in the sailor's cap."

"Then why did he tell us we should leave a note for Peter?"

"That's the clincher as far as I'm concerned. If he hadn't said anything, one of us would have thought of it, written a note and slipped it under Peter's door. But when *he* suggests it, he can say, 'Give it to me and I'll slip it under his door.' "

"But of course he didn't."

"No."

"That means that no one knows where we've gone or with whom."

"That's right. He was careful to see that we went out through the café so that not only did no one see us leave, but no one knows that he was there."

"Nice, isn't it?"

"Yes. Does it scare you?"

Sara thought about it seriously for a moment.

"A little. At first I thought it was fun. But now . . . Well, after all, someone did kill Benny the Monk."

"I know. But somehow I don't think anyone would want to kill us. Why should they?"

"If it comes to that, why should they kidnap us? But I think you're right. I don't think anyone is going to want to kill us. And anyway, there are two of us. I mean, neither of us is alone. That helps."

"Yes. And of course there's Peter. If anyone can find us, he will."

"That's the biggest thing of all. Where do you think they're taking us?"

"Let's see." Andrew kneeled on the cushions of the locker and looked out through one of the portholes on the port side. "We're on the East River going north. At least I think . . . Yes. There's Blackwell's Island ahead. Of course they can stop anywhere along here, on either the Manhattan or the Long Island City side. But if they don't, if they keep going—and somehow I think they will—then they can either go up the Long Island Sound or over to the Hudson by way of Spuyten Duyvil."

"I suppose the door really is locked."

"I'm sure it is. I heard Manion lock it, but . . ." He pulled on it. "It's locked all right."

"Shall we bang on it and yell and make a fuss?"

"A little late for that, isn't it?" He thought a minute. "No. Let them wonder why we're *not* making a fuss."

"All right." She yawned. "I'm suddenly sleepy."

"Well, it's after twelve and we've had a pretty big day. If there was something we could do, we'd do it. But since there isn't, I think we should get some sleep."

"All right. See you in the morning." She stretched out on the starboard locker, put a cushion under her head as a pillow and was asleep almost immediately.

Andrew stretched out on the cushions of the port

locker but he didn't fall asleep quite so quickly. He had asked Sara if she were frightened and the truth was that he had been himself. And why not, when, as Sara had pointed out, you remembered Benny the Monk? Though talking about it had helped, he was still anxious. And puzzled. Who had kidnapped them and why? Luckily his mother was away so she wouldn't know about it— at least, not right away. But of course Wyatt would. And while he'd certainly do something about it, (Do what? Notify the police? Try to track them down himself?) he *would* worry. Was there anything Andrew could do to help him, leave some kind of clues that would tell him where they were? That was difficult right now when he was on a boat and didn't know where they were going. But he should be aware of their route so he'd know where they were when they got there.

The launch seemed to be changing direction, was pitching and rolling a bit. Andrew got up and looked out the porthole again. There were docks and buildings that looked like warehouses on his side of the river, but they didn't tell him very much. Then they went under a bridge and he saw another one up ahead, and that told him a great deal. They were on the Harlem River, heading for Spuyten Duyvil and the Hudson. If they kept on going, it would be up the Hudson.

He stretched out again, listening to the steady, rhythmic sound of the engine, punctuated by the occasional scrape of a shovel, rattle of coal and clang of the firebox door. Once or twice he heard the toot of a tugboat whistle. And trying to interpret the sounds, visualize their route, he fell asleep.

When Andrew woke, the launch was still chugging along smoothly and steadily. The hanging oil lamp had gone out but light was coming in through the portholes. Sara was awake also, kneeling on the cushions on the other side of the table and looking out of one of the starboard portholes.

"Good morning," he said with deliberate formality.

"Oh, hello."

"Where are we?"

"That's what I'm trying to see, but I can't tell."

Andrew took out his watch. It was a few minutes after six. Then he looked out of his porthole. There was a good deal of fog on the surface of the river, but it was starting to lift; and far off, edging the west bank of the river, he could see high, rocky cliffs.

"Well, we're on the Hudson. I thought that was where we were heading last night. Now I'm sure of it."

"That's what I thought too. Do you know where?"

"We're up pretty far. Those cliffs are much taller than the Palisades. I think they're called the Highlands."

She nodded. "I wonder how much farther we're going. I hope not too far."

"Why?"

"I'm hungry."

He smiled. "So am I. Maybe they'll give us something to eat before we get to wherever we're going." Then as she sat up straighter, her eyes widening, "What is it?"

"If I told you, you wouldn't believe me. Come and look."

He went around the table, kneeled on the locker next to her and looked out. They were much closer to the eastern than the western bank of the river, and the terrain on this side was quite different. The land was sloping, with trees growing almost to the water's edge; in the distance it rose gradually to higher ground. But that's not what Sara was looking at. Some distance ahead of them was an island that was about a quarter of a mile from shore. And on the island was a castle.

Andrew blinked and looked again. They had seen several small imitation castles since they had come to America. The Belvedere in Central Park was one; at least it was built of stone and had a lookout tower. But this seemed to be the real thing. It was, in any case, as large as an English castle, with crenellated ramparts and a tower that looked like a donjon keep. However, there was something a little wrong with its proportions and also its color. Then, as they drew closer, they could see that though it followed the plan and had the general appearance of a castle, with a gatehouse complete with arrow slits and machicolations, unlike a true castle it was built partly of stone and partly of brick.

"I've heard of castles that were actually brought over

here and set up again," said Andrew. "But this is different. It's someone's idea of what a castle looks like."

"I wonder whose?" said Sara. "Who lives there?"

Andrew shrugged. Then as the launch turned and began going in toward shore, they looked at one another.

"Do you think . . .?" asked Sara.

"Maybe."

The launch turned the other way—toward the eastern
side of the island where there was a boathouse and a
dock—then slowed up as the engine was throttled down.

"Yes," said Andrew. "That seems to be where we're
going."

"Then we should find out who does live there."

There was a big man standing on the dock. Manion,
up in the bow, threw him a line and he looped it around
a pile. The engine was reversed and the launch swung
in against the dock and was tied up. Sara and Andrew
jumped down off the locker, stretched and were waiting
when the cabin door was unlocked and opened. The
man with the seaman's cap looked in, jerked his head at
them and they came out into the open cockpit. When
they saw him together with the man who had been on
the dock, they realized that they must be brothers, for
they looked very much alike; both big and strong with
flat faces, snub noses and greyish green eyes.

Manion was up forward, and when the man with the
seaman's cap jerked his head at the dock, he came back
and helped Sara up on to it.

"Thanks," she said. "Where are we going?"

"Up there," he said, nodding toward the castle. "The house."

"Good."

They went up the dock to a gravel path that led toward the castle, Manion walking beside Sara and Andrew but keeping his distance, not really looking at them, and the two big men walking behind them.

"Nice day," said Sara pleasantly.

"Yes," said Manion awkwardly.

"I've been meaning to ask you, how are your children?"

"My children?"

"Yes. When you came to see us that first time, didn't you say that if you'd realized we were there you'd never have dropped that load of cargo because you had children of your own?"

"Look, I didn't like this, lying to you that way and getting you to the launch so you could be shanghaied, but . . ."

"You talk too much, Manion," said the man in the sailor's cap. "Shut up!"

"Who are you telling to shut up?"

"You," said the other big man. "Sven tell you, and I tell you too."

"Well, I don't take orders from you. I take them from just one man, the boss."

Nevertheless, he became quiet, didn't say another word to Sara and Andrew, just walked sullenly beside them up the path to the castle.

II

The Castle

There were several buildings beside the boathouse between the dock and the castle; one was a chicken coop and one looked like a barn. The path circled around them and past a vegetable garden, then went through a flower garden and alongside a terrace to end at the massive front door that faced west toward the river.

The man in the sailor's cap rapped on the door with a heavy iron knocker, and after a moment, it opened and a small black man in a white coat looked out. It was obvious that he was not young, for his face was lined and his closely cropped hair was grey, but he seemed very spry and alert.

"So you're here," he said. "Come in, come in." Then as Sara and Andrew stepped into the stone flagged entrance hall, "I'm Gideon. They didn't tell me your names." He nodded when Sara and Andrew had done so. "Very good. Axel," he said to the big man who had been waiting at the dock, "the boss wants you to wait out here. Sven, you and Manion can go. As for you, Sara and Andrew, will you come this way?" and he led them to an arched opening on the left of the entrance hall.

Beyond it was a large, high-ceilinged room with French doors that opened onto the terrace. At the end of the room was a huge, ornate fireplace. And standing in front of it was Dandy Dan Cady and his companion, Biggs.

"Here are your guests," said Gideon. "If you want me, ring. Meantime I got things to do." And he went into the adjoining dining room and disappeared through a swinging baize door.

"Good morning," said Cady with an easy smile.

"So it was you who had us kidnapped," said Sara. "I suppose we should have known it."

"Now why do you say that? How could you have known?"

"Well, it was almost certain to be someone we knew, not a stranger. And you're the only person we've met since we've been here who's two-faced enough for the job."

"Two-faced?"

"Well, what would you call the way you acted? First you tried to scare our friend Wyatt off. And when you couldn't—and that twister Manion peached on you—you pretended you were coming clean, but, at the same time, you tried to buy Wyatt."

"Well, you certainly do talk straight, don't you?" said Cady laughing.

"Which is more than you do. How did you get Manion to play Judas for you and bring us to the launch?"

"Squeezed him a little where he couldn't take squeezing—he needed a job—and offered him a little something; the old carrot and stick. But if you feel you should have guessed that much, you've probably guessed the rest, why we wanted you."

"Of course," said Andrew. For though, like Sara, it hadn't occurred to him that Cady might be behind the kidnapping, once he knew the truth, it wasn't difficult to decide why. "You want to use us to squeeze him the way you did Manion, get him to find that missing file for you."

"Well, I'll be darned!" said Cady admiringly. "Are all you British naturally smart or did it rub off on you from being with Wyatt?"

"A little of both," said Sara. "What I don't understand is why you think he can find it when neither your private detective nor the police could."

"I told you why when I came to see you. I'm not sure the police *want* to find it. There's too much about them in it. Besides I'm convinced that he's much smarter than either my private detective or the police."

"I don't think there's any question about that," said Andrew. "But he wouldn't have to be very smart to realize—as we should have—that you were behind this. After all, he knows how badly you want the file."

"But that's exactly why he won't suspect me," said Cady, smiling. "He'll refuse to believe I'd be stupid enough to kidnap you when I'd be one of the first people he'd suspect."

"Only *one* of the first?"

"Why, yes. There are any number of people who might grab you to get him to find the file—anyone who's in it and is being blackmailed—or anyone who'd like to *do* some blackmailing."

"And of course if he asked you about it," said Sara, "you'd say you didn't know a thing about it."

"Of course. But in the meantime he can't even ask me because he doesn't know where I am. No one does. No one even knows that I've rented this island. No, he'll think that someone else has you and wants me to be blamed for it, and the simplest thing for him to do if he wants you back is to find the file."

"How are you going to let him know what you want and what he's to do about it?" asked Andrew.

"I've written him a note. You can read it if you like. Here." And he handed him a plain white envelope addressed to Inspector Peter Wyatt.

Andrew took out the note, and he and Sara read it together.

"Dear Inspector," it said. "You don't know who I am, but I know who you are and I also know how much your young friends, Sara and Andrew, mean to you. I have them in a place you will never find. I want the file cabinet that is missing from the State Investigators' office that was burned several months ago. Find it, and they will be returned to you safe and sound. When you have the file, let me know in the so-called agony (Personal) column of the *Herald*. If you wish to communicate with me for any other reason, do so in the same way."

It was written in a careful script, which was completely without character, and it was signed "The Sachem."

"What's a sachem?" asked Sara.

"An Indian chief," said Andrew. "There's just one thing wrong with your letter. How is he going to be sure you really have us?"

"I thought of that," said Cady. "And that's why I showed you the note. I think you should both sign it."

Andrew shook his head. "Signing it isn't enough. Someone could forge our signatures. The only way he'd believe it is if I added something that he knew only I could have written."

Dandy Dan looked at him and then at Biggs.

"What do you think, Biggsy?"

"Don't ask me. You know I've been against the whole thing from the beginning."

"Yes, I know and I don't know why. You're not usually so fussy. All right," he said to Andrew. "We'll try it. Write what you want, and we'll look at it. If it looks okay, we'll send it."

"I'll need a pencil or a pen."

"There's a desk over there," said Cady, nodding to one in the corner near the windows. Andrew walked over to it, thinking harder than he ever had in his life. He knew what he wanted to do, but whether he'd be able to was something else again. He picked up a pen, dipped it into the inkwell, then sat there, still thinking.

"While we're waiting, is there anything the two of you would like?" asked Cady.

"Yes," said Sara promptly. "Some breakfast."

"That's easy," said Cady. "Will you ring for Gideon, Biggsy?"

"Of course," said the little man. He tugged at a bell-pull; a bell tinkled faintly somewhere in the distance; and a moment later the white-coated black man came back in.

"Gideon, we've got a pair of very hungry young people here. Do you think you can do something about it?"

"I reckon maybe I can."

"What would you like for your breakfast, Sara?" asked Cady.

"Why are you asking her?" said Gideon, frowning. "Am I the cook or ain't I?"

"Of course, you're the cook."

"Well, all right then." He turned to Sara. "You willing to leave it to Gideon, little lady?"

"Yes, I am."

"Sure. Because you're smart—anyone can see that." Then, as he turned to go, "By the way, Mr. Biggs, I've been meaning to tell you we need some more coal."

"Heating coal or cooking coal?" asked Biggs.

"Now why would be be needing heating coal at this time of year?"

"All right. I'll order some right away."

"Where?" asked Cady.

"You mean where will I order it? There's a coal dealer in Cold Spring. I'll get it from him. Why?"

"You know very well why. I still haven't gotten over that load you had shipped up here all the way from New York."

"I told you how that happened. We've been dealing with Burke for years. He supplies all the coal we give away over Christmas and Thanksgiving, and he had a barge going up the river to Poughkeepsie anyway. . . ."

"All right, all right." Then, looking over at Andrew, "How are you doing, young fellow?"

"I'm almost finished," said Andrew. He read over what he had written, blotted it and handed it to Cady.

Cady read it and frowned, for this is what Andrew had added to the note.

"As John Henry North said, 'No man is a prisoner save of his own choosing. Every man is a piece of the continent, a part of the main, and any man's loss diminishes me because I am involved in mankind.' Therefore

I urge you to do as our friend the Sachem requests."
And he had signed it, Childe Roland.

"I don't get it," he said. "Is it supposed to mean something? Here, Biggsy. You take a look at it."

Biggs read it carefully, going over it twice.

"As you probably gathered, the British are very literary," he said. "I don't happen to know who this North is. . . ."

"One of our philosophical and religious writers," said Andrew glibly. "He was Dean of Westminster in the early seventeenth century."

"And this Childe Roland, I suppose that's what Wyatt calls you."

"That's right. It's from *King Lear*, kind of a joke."

Biggs nodded. "I don't see anything wrong with it," he said, giving the note back to Cady.

"Well, send it then," said Cady.

"How?" asked Andrew. "When will Wyatt get it?"

"Sven will take Manion over to Cold Spring in the launch, and Manion will take the train down and drop it at the hotel. He should have it before noon. Why?"

"Because I don't want him to worry about us. And I'd also like to know how long we'll have to stay here."

"You think he'll get started on it right away?"

"Of course."

"Then you shouldn't have to stay here too long. In the meantime, we'll do everything we can to make you comfortable. Axel," he called to the big man who was waiting in the entrance hall, "will you take our guests up to their quarters?"

"Sure, boss."

"What about our breakfast?" asked Sara.

"Gideon will bring it up to you," said Cady.

"This way," said Axel, putting one hand on Sara's shoulder and one on Andrew's and pushing them out toward the entrance hall.

"Take your hands off me!" said Sara angrily, slapping his hand away.

"Easy, Axel," said Cady. "You'll have to forgive him," he said to Sara. "He doesn't mean any harm, but I'm afraid he learned his manners in a lumber camp."

"I just know you tell me to watch them," growled Axel. "So that's what I do. Go ahead now," he said to Sara and Andrew. "Up there." And he nodded toward a flight of stairs that led up from the far side of the entrance hall. They began climbing the stairs. At the end of the first flight there was a landing, then it went up again. It continued up—and they continued climbing—until it was clear that they must be in the tower. They were beginning to wonder how high they would have to go when the stairs ended in front of a door. Axel opened it, and they went in. Then, without another word, he pulled the door shut and locked it.

Sara and Andrew exchanged glances. Sara smiled wryly, Andrew shrugged, and they walked forward and looked around.

They were in a large, square, very light room that was, as they had suspected, at the very top of the tower. There were two beds in it with a night table between them. A wash stand with a pitcher and basin on it stood in one corner and in another was a trunk. The only other piece of furniture in the room was a large wardrobe that stood against the wall near the door. Though the room was sparsely furnished, the view was quite remarkable because they were at least sixty feet up and there were windows on three sides, facing north, south and west. The windows to the north looked up the river, the southern windows looked down it, and the western windows looked across the river to the cliffs that Andrew thought were called the Highlands and that were probably the foothills of the Catskill Mountains.

"What did you write in the note to Peter?" asked Sara, walking to one of the north windows and looking out.

Andrew told her. She thought about it for a minute, frowning.

"What does it mean?" she asked.

He told her that, too.

"Oh. Do you think he'll understand?"

"I hope so," he said, joining her at the window. "Quite a view."

"Yes." She looked out of one of the west windows and then one of the south windows. "The island isn't very big." It was roughly square and about a quarter of a mile each way.

"No, it isn't. But it's big enough."

"So that it's not going to be easy to get away, you mean."

"That's right."

"Do you think we *will* be able to get away?"

"I don't know. Let's not talk about it until after Gideon's been here."

"All right. I liked him. At least I liked him more than Cady or Biggs or that Axel ox. But I wish he'd hurry. I really am hungry."

"So am I. It's the sea air that does it."

"Sea?"

"Well, river air—being on a boat."

"I don't even need that. I can be hungry right in a city—either New York or London. And I usually am."

"That's very unladylike, you know. Ladies aren't ever supposed to be hungry. They're just supposed to toy with their food."

"Then isn't it a good thing I'm not a lady."

"What are you?"

"I don't know. Wait a minute." She went to the door and listened. "Yes, he's coming."

Slow footsteps came up the stairs, pausing once or twice for, as the two of them knew, it was quite a long climb. There was a rattle as Gideon set the tray down, unlocked and opened the door. Then he came in, holding it in front of him.

"Well, this is a fine thing," he said, looking around for a table on which to set the tray. "How do they expect you young people to eat?"

"You complain to them when you go back downstairs," said Sara. "Meanwhile, here." She moved the night table between the beds down nearer the foot. "What about this?"

"It'll have to do," said Gideon, setting the tray down on it. "Now go ahead and eat while it's still hot."

Whatever it was he was talking about was concealed by a silver cover, one on each plate. Sara and Andrew each sat down on a bed and removed one of the silver covers.

"Pancakes!" said Sara softly. "And bacon."

"Not just pancakes, blueberry pancakes. I picked the blueberries this morning. I'm going to give them to the boss and Mr. Biggs for lunch, but I figured they could spare a few for your pancakes." He watched as they buttered the pancakes and poured golden syrup over them. "Well?" he asked as they each tasted their first forkful. "Is it good?"

"Good?" said Andrew. "Gideon, you're doing yourself a grave injustice. We'll have to come up with a brand new word to describe them."

"Scrumptious," said Sara. "Or perhaps frabjous."

"Frabjous," said Gideon, chuckling. "That's a good one. Where'd you get that?"

"From a poem we both like," said Andrew. " 'O

frabjous day! Callooh! Callay! He chortled in his joy.' "

"Well, I guess you like them all right," said Gideon. "But now do you see why I didn't want anyone to tell me what to fix?"

"We certainly do," said Sara. "But I can't help wondering what you're going to do for an encore."

"What's an encore?"

"She means what you're going to give us for lunch," said Andrew.

"I don't know myself yet. I'll have to think about it. If we were back down home, I'd go out and catch a mess of catfish. You ever eat catfish?"

"No," said Sara.

"They're pretty frabjous, too. Well, like I said, I'll think about it."

"Do you do all the cooking yourself?" asked Sara.

Andrew knew what she was doing. She was trying to find out exactly how many people there were in the castle. And so, while he tried to look casual and continued eating, he listened to Gideon's answer with interest.

"All the cooking *and* the cleaning. We used to have two ladies come out from Cold Spring to do the cleaning and help out all around. But the boss stopped that a couple of days ago—I guess because he doesn't want anyone to know you two are here."

"How do you feel about that—his keeping us prisoners here?" asked Andrew.

"I don't like it—I don't think it's right—but I'm sure

Mr. Cady's got his reasons for it. In any case, you won't come to no harm. He's not a bad man, Mr. Cady. And neither is Mr. Biggs. He's quiet, but very smart. Mr. Cady counts on him for a lot."

"What about that other pair, Axel and Sven?" asked Sara.

"The Hansen brothers? I don't have much truck with them. Sven runs the boat and Axel takes care of the grounds and anything that needs fixing in the house. I guess they're all right." Then, leaning closer to the two young people. "No, they're not. To tell you the truth, I don't like 'em. They're *mean!*"

"We don't like them either," said Andrew. "But we won't tell anyone how you feel about them."

"Wouldn't do any of us any good," said Gideon. Then, looking at their empty plates, "Well, I guess you were pretty hungry at that."

"Even if we hadn't been, we still wouldn't have left anything," said Sara. "It was delicious."

"Glad you think so. I like cooking for people who appreciate it. Drink your milk now, and I'll take the tray." Then, as they did so, "That's it. It was nice talking to you. I'll see you again at lunchtime." And picking up the tray, he went out, locking the door behind him.

"Well, now we know how many people we have to worry about," said Andrew. "When Manion leaves, there'll be five—Cady, Biggs, Gideon and the two Hansens."

"What about the man who was stoking the fire on the launch?"

"I forgot about him. That makes six. But the major problems remain the same—how to get out of this room and how to get off the island. Let's look around a bit."

"The room or the island?"

"Both. The island first."

They went back to the north window and looked out. The castle was near the southern end of the island, and to the north, beyond the gardens, were some carefully spaced trees—probably an orchard—and beyond that a small but dense wood. To the east, as much as they could see, was the dock, boathouse, chicken coop and the building that looked like a barn. The only thing they hadn't seen or noticed before was a rowboat that was pulled up on the shore on the southeast corner of the island.

"I wonder what that boat's doing there," said Andrew. "Why it's not at the boathouse."

Sara looked at it thoughtfully. "I'll bet it's Gideon's," she said. "He asked if we liked catfish. He probably likes to fish, and, if he does, he'd keep the boat there where it's nearer the kitchen and handier than if it were at the boathouse."

"I've a feeling you're right," said Andrew. Looking at it more closely, he could see that it was heavy and rather clumsy, as if it had been made by a local carpenter rather than at a boatyard like the launch. "But that's

volume two. Let's see how we do with volume one."
And he went over to look at the door.

It took only a minute to convince him that there was
very little that they could do there. The door was heavy
and the lock was a new Yale, as efficient as their own
British Chubb locks.

"Do you think you can pick it?" asked Sara.

"No. It would take a professional with very good
tools to do that. What's in the trunk?"

"Probably blankets and linen."

She was right. There were several blankets in the
trunk and under them sheets, pillow cases, towels and
other articles of household linen.

"What about the wardrobe?" asked Andrew.

"Old clothes," said Sara. And again she was right,
though the clothes were probably not exactly what she
expected. For, along with the ladies' dresses, coats and
cloaks, there were several military uniforms, rather worn
and stained, probably dating from the War Between the
States. They took out some of the clothes and looked
behind them to see if they could find anything useful,
but there was nothing there but some old shoes and
boots.

"Doesn't look very good, does it?" said Andrew.

"No. What if we made a rope out of sheets or blankets, hung it out the window and slid down that?"

"I've read about that, but I'm not sure I know how to
do it. Do you?"

"No. I imagine you tear the blankets or sheets into strips and twist or braid them to make them stronger."

"And what if they're not strong enough? We're pretty far up."

"Well, we wouldn't try sliding down it until we'd tested it, made sure it would hold our weight."

"Have you ever slid down a sixty foot rope?"

"No. Have you?"

"Not sixty feet, but I've climbed up and down a twelve foot rope at school, and it's not easy, especially when the bottom end is loose and whips around. I suppose I could go down first and hold it for you, but even then, where would we be? We'd still be out here on the island and have to figure out some way to get ashore."

"There are boats."

"What boats? The launch?"

"No. I don't suppose we could handle that. But what about that rowboat of Gideon's?"

"Which the launch could catch in no time at all when they discovered we were gone."

"But if we did it at night, they wouldn't know we were gone until morning. Wouldn't that give us time to get ashore—even in Gideon's rowboat?"

"Maybe."

She frowned at him. "Are you saying we shouldn't do anything about this? Shouldn't even try to escape?"

"I did try to do something about it. I wrote that note to Peter. As for the suggestions you've been making, will you give me a few minutes to think about them?"

"All right."

He went over to a window and looked out. It was like Sara to refuse to accept the situation they were in, to immediately start thinking about what they could do about it. On the other hand, he was older than she was and more practical, and he was very conscious of the risks they would run if they did what she was proposing. He looked down at the ground so far below and a chill came over him. He wouldn't like to climb down all that distance on an improvised rope. He wasn't sure that even a sailor, used to both heights and ropes, would feel comfortable about it. And still, there must be something they could do, and, if there was, he wanted to do it because he was no more willing than Sara was to just sit back and wait until they were either rescued or released. Then, suddenly, his eyes widened. He turned and looked at the door, at the wardrobe. And he grinned.

"You've thought of something," said Sara.

"Yes."

"What is it?"

He told her.

"Andrew, that's wonderful!" she said, her eyes shining. "When do we do it?"

"It's going to take a while to get ready. What about tomorrow night after supper?"

"All right. And in the meantime?"

"We've got to make them think that we're perfectly

happy to stay here. That all we've got on our minds is how to spend the time."

And so when Gideon came back with their lunch, Sara said, "Gideon, there's no telling how long we're going to be here. Can't you get us some books to read or some kind of game we could play?"

"You mean like cards?"

"Well, yes. Cards would do."

"I got a better idea. How about checkers?"

"Checkers would be fine."

"I think I saw some in the parlor. I'll talk to the boss about it."

They ate their lunch, which consisted of cold ham and potato salad with freshly made hot biscuits; and when Gideon came back up to collect their dishes he brought a box of checkers, a board and a copy of Hawthorne's *The Scarlet Letter*. Sara and Andrew thanked him for the lunch, the game and the book, and when he had left and they were fairly sure they would not be disturbed, they went to work.

They had decided that sheets would be better for their purpose than blankets and took four of them out of the trunk. Andrew began tearing them in strips and giving the strips to Sara. Sara twisted several strips together, then began braiding them. It was fairly slow work at first, but when Andrew finished tearing the sheets, he started braiding them too, and by late afternoon they had about forty feet of improvised rope finished. They tested it by tying one end of it to the doorknob and throwing the rest of it over the wardrobe. Andrew climbed up it, and it held his weight so they were satisfied with that aspect of it. They had looked out of the window some time before and discovered that their guess about the rowboat was correct. Gideon had gone out in it, anchored a short distance off the end of the island and spent most of the afternoon fishing.

When he began to row back to the island, the young people decided they had better stop what they were doing, so they coiled the rope they had finished, hid it in the wardrobe, and when Gideon came up with their supper at a little after six, they were engrossed in a checker game.

Gideon watched them for a few minutes, giving Sara advice she did not need for she had won two of the three preceding games. Then, his culinary pride asserting itself, he insisted that they stop and eat their supper while it was still hot. It was southern fried chicken with baked sweet potatoes, followed by apple pie, still warm from the oven. They had no difficulty in eating it all with relish and praising it in a way that satisfied Gideon. He waited until they were finished, asked if they had any further messages or requests for Cady and, when they said they didn't, bade them good night, took the tray and left.

They continued their rope-making by daylight while it lasted and then by lamplight, and, by about eleven o'clock, they had a rope they thought was long enough for their purposes. They let it down out of the western window of their room, which could not be seen from the front of the castle, found that it reached to within a few feet of the ground and, satisfied, pulled it up, coiled and hid it, and went to sleep feeling that they had done a good day's work.

Though they played a good deal of checkers the next day and took turns reading aloud from *The Scarlet Letter*, the time seemed to pass more slowly than it had the previous day, and they waited impatiently for evening.

Gideon came up with their supper at about six thirty, grumbling because the boss and Biggs had decided that they wanted to eat a bit early that night so he'd have to go right back down and take care of them instead of being able to visit for a while with Sara and Andrew. They commiserated with him, but suggested that perhaps he could do so later on when he came back up for their tray.

It was after eight, just beginning to get dark, when he did come back. He unlocked and opened the door, started to go in, then paused staring. One of the southern windows was open, a rope made of torn-up sheets was tied to one of the beds and hung out the window, and Sara and Andrew were gone. He hurried to the window and looked out. The improvised rope dangled lazily with the end within a foot or two of the ground, but there was no sign of the two young people.

"Lordy, Lordy!" moaned Gideon, turning and running back out the door. "Boss, boss!" he called as he ran down the stairs, "We got trouble! Bad trouble!"

12

Escape

The moment Sara and Andrew heard Gideon leave, they came out of the wardrobe where they had been hiding, hurried out through the open door and followed him down the tower stairs. They reached the bottom as he ran into the parlor where Cady and Biggs were having their after-dinner coffee, heard Cady say, "What is it, Gideon? What's wrong?" and heard Gideon answer, "The kids is gone!"

Glancing into the parlor to make sure they were un-observed, Andrew nodded to Sara, and they ran to the outside door, opened it and were outside on the terrace.

"The rowboat now?" whispered Sara.

"Yes. But let's wait a minute, see what they're going to do first."

Sara nodded and crouched down next to him behind the hedge that ran around the terrace.

"That's impossible!" Cady was saying. "Are you telling me that they climbed down from up there?"

"If Gideon says they're gone, they're gone," said Biggs. "When did you last see them?"

"When I brung 'em their supper at about six thirty."

"That means that they've been gone for almost two hours," said Cady. "Damn it all, Biggs, this is your fault! Why the devil didn't you tell me that they were that smart and that tricky?"

"How was I supposed to know it?"

"What do you mean, how? What in blazes do you think I pay you for? Do you realize what kind of trouble we'll be in if they get away?"

"That's not going to be easy. After all, we are on an island."

"Don't you think I know that? They're probably still here, hiding someplace. Gideon, tell the Hansens and have them start searching the grounds! As for you, Biggsy, you start looking up at the northern end, the woods, and . . . no, never mind. I'll do that myself!" And as Gideon hurried back toward the kitchen, Cady opened one of the French doors, came out and went running along the terrace, going toward the northern, wooded part of the island.

Biggs remained where he was for a moment, staring after Cady with a look of such intense anger and resentment that Sara clutched Andrew's hand.

"Did you see that?" she whispered.

"Yes. We'd better go now."

Getting up from behind the hedge, they ran around the tower, past the trailing end of the improvised rope, then south to the tip of the island where Gideon's boat was drawn up on the sandy beach, with the rock that he used as an anchor lying beside it.

"Quick! Help me shove it out!" said Andrew, lifting the rock into the boat.

Together they pushed it out until it was floating free. But now, in spite of their previous discussion, Sara hesitated.

"The oars are in it. Don't you think maybe we could get away this way?"

"If we'd left when they thought we did, yes. But not now. Sven will probably take the launch out, and they'd catch us before we got anywhere near shore."

"All right. Tip it?"

"Yes."

Wading out into the shallow water, they both stood on one gunwale until it dipped under the surface and the boat began to fill. Then they jumped off into the sandy shallows, gave the boat one more push and watched it drift away. Just before it disappeared into the darkness, water filled it completely, and it sank out of sight into the muddy depths of the river.

"Now for the barn," said Andrew as they waded ashore. Together they ran toward the large wooden building they had noticed when they first landed. Just before they reached it, Andrew realized that the sliding doors faced the river, not the castle, and that a wooden ramp sloped down from the doors to the water's edge.

"It's not a barn," he said, pulling one of the sliding doors open. "It's an icehouse. Not that it matters."

"An icehouse?" said Sara slipping through the opening.

"Yes," said Andrew, following her in and pushing the door shut. He gestured toward the pile of sawdust that was some seven or eight feet high. "They cut river ice in the winter, drag it in here and cover it with sawdust to keep it from melting until they want it."

"Won't we freeze if we stay here?"

"Does it feel cold?"

"No. As a matter of fact, it's very comfortable."

"The sawdust acts as a kind of blanket, keeps the warm air from the ice and so the air doesn't get cold. Besides, we're going up there," and he pointed to a crude ladder nailed to the wall that led to a platform over the mound of sawdust.

They climbed the ladder, found some old horse blankets and burlap bags on the platform, which they agreed would be useful either as blankets or to lie on.

"Well, we did it," said Sara, sitting down.

"So far we seem to be all right," agreed Andrew.

"I wonder where they are, what they're doing."

"There's no telling, so we'd better be quiet."

Sara nodded, and they sat there in silence for some

time. Then suddenly, so close to them they both jumped, they heard one of the Hansen brothers exclaim.

"Gideon's boat!" he called out. "They took Gideon's boat!"

"Are you sure?" asked Biggs, slightly further away.

"Come and look. It's gone."

"All right. You tell Sven and I'll tell the boss. He'll probably want you both to go looking for them in the launch."

"Some chance of finding them with the head start they've got, especially now that it's dark," grumbled Hansen. "But all right."

"Well, you were right about the boat," whispered Sara. "If we'd taken it, they would have caught us. But now we're safe. Because if they think we're gone, they'll stop looking for us here, won't they?"

"Yes. As I said, so far we're all right. Of course what we'll do tomorrow is something else again."

"How we'll get off the island, you mean."

"Yes."

"Do you have any ideas about that?"

"A few."

"Like what?"

"Well, if they don't find us on the river tonight—and of course they won't—they'll probably go off looking for us in the launch again tomorrow. And if they do . . . . Well, I'd like to take a look in the boathouse."

"You mean there may be another boat there."

"Yes."

It was completely dark in the upper part of the ice-house where they sat side by side on the pile of sacks and old blankets, too dark for Sara to see his face. But she knew him well enough so that she could read his voice as easily as his expression.

"All right," she said. "What is it?"

"What's what?"

"You're not thinking about tomorrow, about getting away. You're thinking about something else."

"Yes. About the look on Biggs' face when Cady yelled at him and then went off."

"He doesn't like Cady very much."

"It's more than that. Much, much more."

"Yes, I know. But doesn't that happen fairly often when you're working for someone and don't feel that they're treating you the way they should?"

"That you feel *that* violent?"

"I don't know. And I don't know what you're getting at. Is there something else?"

"Yes. If you wanted to bring something up here from New York and you didn't want anyone to know about it, how could you do it?"

She sat there, smelling the pungent, woody smell of the sawdust, listening to the sough of the night wind and the soft splash of the waves in the river and thinking. She knew that, like Wyatt, Andrew always played fair. If either of them asked you a question, you should be able to answer it. And then it came to her, not just the question he had asked, but the answer to a much more important one. Clutching him excitedly, she told him.

"Good girl. That's what I think too."

"What are we going to do about it?"

"Before we leave here, I'd like to find out if we're right."

"Now?"

"No. Everyone's too worked up about our escaping, and there's no telling when they'll go to sleep. But maybe early tomorrow morning."

"All right."

"Are you warm enough?"

"Yes. The thing is—I'm ashamed to say it, but I'm hungry."

"We had supper before we escaped."

"I know. But I was so excited that I gobbled it. And besides, quite a few things have happened since. I know that there's nothing we can do about it . . ."

"No? Here."

"What is it?"

"What does it feel like?"

"Bread!"

"That's right. Gideon's homemade bread. I was too excited to eat it at supper too, but I thought we might want it later on, so I stuck it in my pocket."

"Andrew, you think of everything!"

"No, I don't. I'm not Peter—and I'm sure that not

even he does."

It was a little after five when they awoke. Andrew opened his eyes, stretched, glanced at his watch, then saw that Sara was awake too and looking at him.

"Hi," he said. "How are you?"

"Stiff."

"Me too. We'll be all right when we start moving."

"Are we going to see if our guess last night was right?"

"Are you game?"

"Of course."

"Let's go, then."

Throwing off the old horse blankets, they climbed down the ladder, slid open the icehouse door and looked out. Though the sun was not yet up, the night was gone and everything was suffused with a pearly, before-dawn light. They listened, but could hear nothing but the sleepy clucking of the chickens in the chicken coop, the faint splashing of the river waves on the sandy beach. Reassured, they stepped out and, walking softly, rounded the corner of the icehouse. The only light on in the castle was in a room next to the kitchen, probably Gideon's room.

"Shall we take a chance on it?" asked Sara.

"I think so. He probably just got up and isn't dressed yet."

She nodded and they tiptoed to the back of the castle. Next to the kitchen door was an areaway with three steps leading down to the cellar door.

"I'll go down," whispered Andrew. "You wait here and keep watch."

"Why do I have to stay here?"

"So you can warn me if Gideon comes out or someone else comes along."

She hesitated, then nodded.

He went down the steps to the cellar door and tried the knob. The door wasn't locked and he eased it open. The cellar was large and cavernous, but what he was interested in lay close at hand. To the left of the steps was a large open bin with loose coal in it. In front of the bin was a shovel and a coal scuttle. This was probably the cooking coal that Gideon had been talking about. To the right of the steps, under the dusty window, was a much larger storage area that was piled high with coal sacks. Andrew peered through the spaces between the slats that formed the wall of the storage area, but could see nothing but the sacks.

He opened the door that led into it and, bending down, forced his hand between the coal sacks. He felt something, and separating the sacks, he saw that there was a packing case buried under them. A packing case. That wasn't what he had been looking for. Still, maybe he should look into it. But before he could even start to do so, he lost his opportunity.

There was an exclamation outside, Sara called, "Nommus, Andrew! Chickie! Run!" and there was the sound of running feet. Slamming the storage door, Andrew ran up the steps. Like a mother bird trying to draw a fox away from her hidden nest, Sara was running back toward the icehouse, still calling and pretending that Andrew was somewhere over there. And running after her was Axel Hansen. Fleet as she was, his legs were too long for her. Reaching out, he caught her by her flying hair and pulled her to a stop.

"Ow!" she cried. "You pongy abishag!"

As he took a firmer grip on her, Andrew threw himself upon him. He punched him as hard as he could in the stomach, kicked him in the ankle.

"Let her go, you po-faced bully!" he said furiously.

Hansen hit him once, backhanded, and knocked him to the ground. Then, bending down, he hauled him to his feet, holding him with one hand and Sara with the other.

"Boss, boss!" he shouted. "I got 'em, got both of them!"

The Mask Removed

"So you never left the island after all," said Cady.

It was about fifteen minutes later and he was sitting at the desk in the castle parlor wearing a wine-colored dressing gown. Biggs, dressed as usual in his dark suit and stiff white collar, was there too, and so was Gideon. The only member of the company who was not there was Sven Hansen.

"I said, so you never left the island," repeated Cady.

Angry and chagrined, Sara and Andrew said nothing, and their silence must have annoyed Axel, who stood behind them, watching them.

"When the boss talks to you," he growled, poking Andrew in the back, "you answer!"

Controlling his anger, Andrew did not turn, still said nothing.

"It's all right, Axel," said Cady. "They don't have to

say anything if they don't want to. The big thing is that, thanks to you, we've got them again. And the only question is where we can keep them so they won't give us any more trouble."

"Where I want to put them in the first place," said Axel. "Down in the cellar!"

"That's no good, boss," said Gideon. "In fact, that's bad!"

"Why bad?" said Axel.

"I told you why the first time we all talked about it," said Gideon. "Because the cellar's dark and cold and damp, and if you keep them there for more than a day or so, you're going to have a pair of sick chickens on your hands!"

"So where you want to keep them?" asked Axel.

"In the storeroom next to the kitchen."

"So you can talk to them any time you want, right?"

"Well, what's wrong with that?"

"What's wrong," said Axel, "is that if they can get out from room in tower, why can't they get out from storeroom?"

"Because it'll be easier to watch them there," said Gideon. "And because we'll nail the windows shut. And if that doesn't satisfy you, you stubborn squarehead—"

"Who you calling a squarehead?" said Hansen angrily.

"All right, you two, that's enough," said Cady.

"Actually, it's all academic," said a new voice. "Because no one's going to lock them up anywhere."

Sara and Andrew both turned, and as Wyatt came in through the French doors they ran over to him.

"We knew you'd come!" said Sara, hugging him. "Golly, we're glad to see you!"

"And I to see you," said Wyatt, looking at them searchingly. "Are you all right?"

"They are, but you won't be if you try anything!" said Cady. Recovering from his surprise, he had taken a revolver from his desk drawer and now held it levelled at Wyatt, "So don't move. Frisk him, Axel!"

"You should know better than that," said Wyatt, as Hansen ran his hands over his pockets." English policemen don't carry guns."

"Well, this isn't England," said Cady, relaxing somewhat. "You didn't come here alone, did you?"

"What? No, of course not."

"He's lying!" said Biggs, who had been watching him intently.

"How do you know?"

"If any cops came with him, where are they? It would be just like him to come alone, just as it is for him to come without a gun."

"I've got a feeling you're right," said Cady, putting the revolver down on the desk. "Just for fun, do you want to tell us how you found us?"

"That should be obvious," said Wyatt. "Andrew told me where you were in his note."

"That's what I figured. Again, just for fun, would

you spell it out for us?"

"If you like. Do you remember what he wrote?"

"Not really."

"Well, in what he claimed was a quotation from one John Henry North he said something about no man being a *prisoner*. There is no John Henry North, but there was a John Donne and what followed made it clear that he was quoting from the *Devotions* in which Donne said, 'No man is an *island*.' The North would have been puzzling if it had not been supplemented by the Henry, but together they gave me North River and Henry Hudson, so I then had an island in the Hudson. As to which one, the clue to that lay in the way it was signed. Do you remember that?"

"Childe Roland, wasn't it?" said Biggs.

"Right. The quotation there was from Browning. 'Childe Roland to the dark tower came.' So there it was. It didn't take much research to discover that there was an island in the Hudson on which there was a dark tower. Or, to be more precise, a sham castle."

"Well, well," said Cady. "Now do you see the value of a British education, Biggsy?" Then, as Biggs smiled mirthlessly, "I must say I admire you both for the way you played this particular game. But the fact is, you've handed me a real problem, Inspector."

"And what's that?"

"You know why I took the kids. To get you to find that file cabinet for me. But now that you're here, I don't know quite what to do. I mean, how can I push you to look for it when—"

"You don't have to," said Andrew, deciding to take a chance on it. "I can tell you where it is."

"The file cabinet?"

"Yes. It's right here in a packing case, hidden under the coal in the cellar."

With surprising and catlike speed, Biggs pounced, grabbed Cady's revolver from the top of the desk and raised it.

"No one move!" he said flatly. "I'll drill the first one who does!"

"Biggsy!" said Cady, staring at him in astonishment. "You mean it was you . . .?"

"Yes, I'm the one who took the file. And used it. And expect to go on using it!"

"But why? How could you? I mean . . ."

"Why?" Biggs laughed bitterly. "If you knew, understood why, maybe I wouldn't have done it. What do they call you? Dandy Dan. And me? Little old Biggsy. Meaning little old nothing! How many years have we been working together? Over ten! Yes, for more than ten years I've been doing most of the thinking and planning—and all the dirty work—and it's still Dandy Dan, the big wheel, boss of the Tenth Ward—and little old Biggsy. Dandy Dan takes all the bows and the shekels, lives high on the hog, and what does Biggsy get? The scraps, the cat-meat that you're willing to throw me.

Well, I got sick of it, see? I wanted my share of the tenderloin, too. So, after I warned you about the commission's report, told you what would happen if they ever released it, I put a match to their office. And, while I was there, I took the file. Took it and mean to keep it!"

"May I ask how?" said Wyatt.

"I'll be glad to tell you," said Biggs. "First of all, there's this." He swept the gun around the room. "The man with the gun gives the orders—especially when people know he'll use it. And the first people I'll use it on is these two kids that everyone's so worried about. They're coming with me, see? They're going to be my guarantee that nobody makes a wrong move!"

"You wouldn't dare hurt them!" said Cady.

"Yes, he would," said Sara. "After all, he's killed one man already—Benny the Monk."

"That's right, Sara," said Biggs, smiling his mirthless smile. "Out of the mouths of babes. Benny helped me torch the commission office, take the file. Then afterward, when he heard all that talk about it, he tried to put the bite on me, blackmail me. Well, I couldn't have that, so I took care of him. But that's enough talk. Gideon, you and Axel go on outside and wait there. You're going to get the file cabinet and carry it down to the dock for me."

"Yes, Mr. Biggs," said Gideon, and he and Axel went out through the French door, paused outside on the terrace.

"You two kids go next," said Biggs. "And while I know you're smart, I'd advise you not to try any tricks."

Sara and Andrew looked at him, at Wyatt, then went out through the French doors too.

"That's fine," said Biggs, edging out after them, the gun ready and his eyes on Wyatt and Cady. "As for the two of you, I'm warning you—" He broke off as a strong hand gripped his wrist and twisted the gun from his grasp.

"You're in no position to warn anyone about anything, Biggsy," said Inspector Decker.

"Where the devil did you come from?"

"Why, we've been here all along," said Decker as half a dozen policemen came up on to the terrace from the garden and from around the corner of the castle. "My friend Wyatt asked to be allowed to go in first to see what was what. But once we found out what we wanted to know, I thought I'd better take over. Because, clever as he is, he's only a visitor and has no jurisdiction here."

"I didn't think you'd be foolish enough to come out here alone," said Andrew to Wyatt, who had joined them.

"Well, I'm glad you didn't say so. How did you know the file cabinet was in the cellar?"

"I'd like to know that too," said Cady, who had come out onto the terrace with Wyatt.

"I just put some things together," said Andrew. "A look on Biggs' face and that coal he had sent up here from New York."

"You mean that's how he got the file cabinet up here?" Cady shook his head admiringly. "It seems to me I owe someone around here plenty."

"Because of the file cabinet or Biggsy?" asked Decker.

"Both."

"I'm not surprised you're glad you discovered Biggsy wasn't quite what you thought. But I am surprised that you're glad about the file cabinet; I had a feeling you didn't really want it found."

"Because there's stuff about me in it? I can handle that. What was giving me trouble was the other people in it who were screaming because someone was putting the bite on them. So I'm relieved. That's why I say I figure I owe someone here plenty."

"So do I," said Decker. "And I'm afraid it's the visiting British—particularly the two youngest ones. I'll tell you what, Dan. Let's join forces when we get back to New York and see if we can't figure out some way of showing our appreciation."

"I always hoped you and I could make a deal about something, Sam," said Cady. "And I can't think of one I'd like better than that."